Mistletoe at the Mill

The Enchanted Mill Series

Book Three

By

C. E. Davis

www.publishnation.co.uk

In Memory of

June Marion Wood

(Nee Collins)

1934 to 2023

Best Mum Ever x

<u>*Cast of characters*</u>

- Cathy Collins - *Genealogist with an online crystal store*
- Sally Buckley – *Maternal Grandma*
- Adam – *Cathy's boyfriend*
- Uncle John Collins – *Paternal Uncle*
- Audrey and Charles Jones – *Maternal Aunt and Uncle*
- Roger Davies – *Cathy's Solicitor*
- Harold Butterworth - *Mill Owner*
- Gillian Bradshaw, *second wife of Martin Bradshaw*
- Fluffy / Oskar - *Scruffy ginger tomcat – Cathy's familiar*
- June and Kenneth Collins – *Parents deceased.*
- Marion and Sydney Collins – *Paternal grandparents deceased.*
- Sam Buckley – *Maternal great grandfather*

<u>*New Coven members*</u>

- Kim Smithies
- Wendy Smithies
- Harold Butterworth

- Roger Davies
- Margaret Gartside – *Hawkeye, her owl familiar*
- Edith Stanworth
- Betty Barratt
- Desdemona Jones - *Mentor of Donna Maria*
- Mary Hanks
- Becki Armstrong
- Inese Jones
- Elizabeth Jones
- Gillian Bradshaw - *Marley, her familiar*
- Clara Jane Holroyd
- Pearl and Ruby

Others

- Brian (Adam father) - *The Magical Police Agency (MPA)*
- Stephen and Hamish - *His blind familiar*
- Alphin and Alderman - *Giants*
- Rimmon and Rowen – *Water nymphs*
- Peter and Susie- *the County Archaeologist and his wife*
- David and Nigel - *Archaeologists and brothers*
- Ulysses – The Cellar Dweller – *A boggart*

- The Goblins – Gordo, Grengo, Gerfo, Glenk and Gloof

- Tamara and Barney– *Adam's Ex and son*

- Mel and Bob – *Tamara's sister and husband*

- Rob and Liv – *Adam's brother and girlfriend*

- Tomasz De Wode - *Vampire*

- Fillipe De Wode – *Vampire*

- Dumar and Franziska De Wode - *Vampires*

- Mikael and Izaak De Wode - *Vampires*

- Gabriel and Adebayo – *Canal Ghosts*

- Ester and Ruth – *Museum Ghosts*

Northwest Coven Leaders

- Monika - Manchester and Salford

- Olwyn - Liverpool

- Theresa - Chester

- Linda - Warrington

- Nikki - Preston

- Jeannette - Lancaster

- Lisa - Carlisle

- Glynis - Upper Valley

- Bronwen - Nether Valley

Special thanks to the members of John Lees Barclay James Harvest and Keith & Monika – JLBJH website hosts.

Also, many thanks to Glynis for proofreading.

Contents

Chapter 1

The Vampire's Lair

Overnight the quiet old textile mill came alive. Cathy walked through the maze of corridors in the mill, she now called her home. She was taken aback by the level of the noise coming from some of the workshop / units.

Since she had come to the mill, the corridors had been noticeably quiet. Cathy had often wondered who was behind the closed shutters, as she had walked these corridors over the last few months.

She thought to herself, how lucky she was that she had inherited the luxury apartment at the mill, from the estate of her deceased maternal Grandma, Sally Buckley. She had only met her Grandma on rare occasions, when she had been alive, because her parents had taken her from Green Valley. Cathy had shown at an early age what a powerful witch she would be. But for her own good, she had been bound from her witchcraft. Sadly, her parents had died in a tragic accident, and Cathy had been raised by her paternal, Uncle John. So, the witchcraft had laid hidden and dormant, until her grandma had passed away.

With the apartment came a workshop / unit that she used for the online crystal store. But also, Cathy had quickly learnt that her normal life would not exist much, now that she was the Head Witch of the Circle of the Dove Stone Coven.

Yes, she had inherited the power of witchcraft, and learnt about the ancestry of the females in her family genealogy. To say it was a shock, was an understatement, Cathy too, had inherited her great grandfather, Sam Buckley's skill of being the Ghost Whisperer of Green Valley.

Over the months Cathy had been in training to be the Head or Leader of the Coven, her grandma's ghost had helped her with her lessons. The magic had flooded back into Cathys life, as quick as it had been bound as an infant.

Cathy continued her journey to CJ's café. Named in honour of Clara Jane, the young ghost that had been freed from her concrete grave in the old lift shaft, by Cathy, when she first came to the mill. Clara Jane had been reunited with her parents but had decided she was staying on as a ghost in the Enchanted Mill; rather than pass over, to who actually knows where one passes over to.

Cathy had been told by her grandma Sally, and her boyfriend, Adam, (of the magical police agency), that the mill became alive at Christmas. But it was only mid-October, way too soon for that. She had briefly visited the cellar, with Oskar, her familiar, in her shapeshifted body of Tiddles the black cat. There she had meet Ulysses, the cellar dweller, the Keeper of the Closed Portal. The thought of being the Keeper of the Open Portal, and responsibility for Christmas, was something that Cathy was still learning about. She carried on walking down the long corridor, from the apartment to the main reception, and the top yard, where the newly opened café was now situated. Two of the new young witches, from the coven had asked to open a café, and Harold had been more than delighted. It had been a hit from day one. Some of the old reclusive men, that had apartments on the top floor of the mill, now met up each morning and seemed to enjoy getting together with their old friends. Adam's grandfather, Stephen and his blind cat, Hamish, seemed to have taken up residency in the café.

Hamish was Stephen's old, blind familiar; the brother of Cathy's familiar, the large ginger tomcat, named Oskar. Who had a mind of his own and was originally Sally's familiar.

"Good morning, Stephen," Cathy said as she joined him at the same table. "How are you today?"

"Extremely well Cathy, you have turned this old mill into a joyous place." The eccentric old man smiled at her, as she gave old Hamish a good tickle.

"Morning, Cathy," The rich voice of old Hamish spoke to Cathy. It had taken a while for Cathy to get her head around cats and dogs talking to her. As well as Oskar and Hamish, they had a sister called Hannah. Gillian, (Cathy's ex-husband's second wife) also had Marley, her whippet as her familiar. Margaret, from the coven had her owl familiar, Hawkeye.

"Good morning, lovely Hamish, and how are you today," Cathy smiled at the old cat, who was in his usual perch, on Stephens knee. "I am here to meet Adam. The café is so busy these days?"

"It is a marvellous place, I haven't been out of my apartment, so much for years." Stephen laughed. "Morning grandson number one," he said to Adam as he saw him walk through the door.

"Good morning, Grandad, how are you and Hamish. Hi Cathy," Adam smiled as he sat down and took a big drink from the latte, Cathy had already ordered him.

"Cathy, I got a call from Monsieur Tomasz last night." Adam told her.

"Who is Monsieur Tomasz?" Cathy asked, having never heard the name before.

"You remember when you asked about the cellar being a vampire's lair? I said no, they have their own place." Adam laughed.

"Really? I thought you were joking. But I am learning now about joking at the supernatural's. Anything is possible at the enchanted mill." Cathy laughed.

"Well, they do exist, and these three are a family of three brothers. They live in the old house, at the other end of the Dove Stone Lake. The old Ash Way Towers. They originally came over from Romania, via France. They are Tomasz, Fillipe and Dumar and his family. They are nice guys, all look to be in their thirties, but no one knows their actual age. Anyway, they have heard you are now in charge here, so they want a meeting with you." Adam explained.

"Why would they want to meet with me?" Cathy asked nervously. "Do they want to taste my blood?"

Chortling, Adam laughed, "not at all, they have their own supplies of blood. Your ancestors set them up with a unique way of serving their cravings. When they arrived in the Valley, the livestock and population needed a way to be kept safe. Your ancestor was the way. So, like Alf and Eric, they owe your family their loyalty. Ask your Gran, she always worked closely with them. I can assure you, there is nothing to be afraid of. I think you will get on very well."

"Will they come here, or can they go out in daylight?" Cathy had hundreds of questions in her mind.

"Cathy, stop over thinking. They are proper vampires, who cannot go out in direct sunlight. But I have told them we will visit then this evening, for dinner. The house is protected by a ward, that your ancestor placed on it to keep them safe. You ok for this evening?" Adam asked.

"Yes, if they want. I am nervous already. I have only seen films like Dracula on TV." Cathy said. A few months ago, she would not have dreamed of meeting any vampires. Let alone having dinner with them, but then, she had not been the leader a coven of witches, nor the Lead witch of the Northwest covens.

Adam took out his phone and dialled the number, he had just spoken too.

"Hello, Albers, this is Adam. Monsieur Tomasz rang to invite Cathy and myself to dinner, this evening. Could you let him know, that we will be there for 6.30pm.

"Yes, that will be perfect Adam," agreed Albers, "I will inform the master's at once."

Cathy could only hear one side of the conversation and had no idea who Albers was. She knew Adam would explain after the phone call.

"All set, I have told them we will be there for 6.30pm, is that ok with you?" Adam told her.

"Who were you talking to?" Cathy asked.

"Oh, sorry I forgot to mention." Adam said. "Albers is, well, in old fashioned days, he would be called a butler. He does all the daytime duties. Such as answering the phone, shopping, organising. I guess he would be called their personal secretary or PA. The family sleep through the day, as that is their normal body clock."

"I see now, that makes sense, the housekeep or PA. Do you know what they want to meet me about? Cathy asked.

"No, not really, maybe it is just a chat and catch up after Sally passed on. Why not have a word with her before we leave." Adam laughed, "it is nothing to worry about though."

"Good idea, I will nip back to the apartment and see if she is around. I catch you up in a while." Cathy left the café, to walk back through the mill to her fabulous apartment. (Which was not used much nowadays. because she more or less, lived with Adam.)

"Gran, are you around?" she asked the empty unit. "Gran, I want to ask you about the vampires."

She felt the chilly breeze of her Grandmas ghost circle around her. Slowly, Sally became visible and grinned at her daughter.

"Oh yes, the handsome vampires, have you had your summons?" Sally teased.

"Well Adam got told they want to meet me. What have we got in common with vampires?" she asked.

"One of our ancestors, Jemima Buckley. About 1850, she was the one that introduced the boys to Green Valley. Don't look surprised, an awful lot of the residents of Green Valley are a lot older than they appear. They helped Jemima get out of a scare with some witch haters, so to reward or repay them, she brought them to Green Valley. The house they live in Ash Way Towers, was built for them, in the quiet location at the far end of the lake. She already owned a few of the houses in the valley at the time. But had this house built to keep them away from prying eyes. It was her daughter Susanna, my own Grandma, that started the process of alternative food for them, other than animals and humans.

Over the years, we have all added our own improvements to this particular foodstuff for the vampires. But I do know they are desperate to walk in the sunshine. Before, they were turned, into vampires. They led a normal life, in France, I think. Hence the accents and names. The family was originally Romanian but move to France in the early 1800s. We have looked at many ways for them to see the sunshine, but never quite made the breakthrough. It will now be your turn to help them." Sally smiled as she thought of the three brothers, happy times.

"You will be fine, Cathy. Have a look at the grimoire and see if it brings up anything, The three young men," Sally laughed. "The three young looking men are delightful. They will show you their workrooms and what they are now looking for, with your help. Don't forget, you will be the most powerful witch in the area, one day."

Cathy smiled as she watched her grandma, reminisce about the three vampires. *"Well, that must be a good sign if Gran smiles like that.* Cathy thought.

"Oh, and wear something smart, those three men dress immaculate at all times. And Franziska, the wife of Dumar, is ultra-attractive, and the most wonderful wife and mother. Try your little black dress, I know you have been saving it for an occasion." Sally giggled, "I am glad you have Adam by your side, the vampires are very sexy and dangerous to the single female. Have a read of the grimoire before you go, I am off to see Harold."

Cathy grabbed a coffee and went into the Temple Room. She got her grimoire off the altar and settled at the huge table. The grimoire flew open to a new blank page, one that Cathy had not noticed before. The Buckley Grimoire, gleamed as she held the book, and the pages began to fill with words.

Cathy was excited as she turned the pages and read the new words, appearing before her eyes.

'Jemima Buckley had travelled on an errand, out of Green Valley, and over the moors to Holme Valley. As the sun was setting, a group of witch-haters were harassing her and as she tried to move to her horse and cart, the haters stopped her. They began to spit at her and call her. She wanted to get back over the tops before it went dark, but could not use her magic, in front of the haters.

Suddenly, three very distinguished gents stood in front of her and helped her with her shopping and onto the cart. She offered them a seat on the cart and a trip over the moorlands, to Green Valley. They had been traveling by night, and told her right away they were vampires, and how the daylight effected them.

Jemima was not scared of the three men; they had saved her from a very unpleasant situation. She told them, they could travel with her, and rest in safety for a few days, if they so desired.

Jemima brought them back to Green Valley and let them stay in one of the inner units at the mill, so no sunlight would get in. The vampires had stayed a lot longer than expected and with the help of Jemima the Ash Way Towers had been built. Over the years, the coven lead by Cathy's family had created the substitute food. Many attempts had been made to create a suitable amulet, or button to allow them to live a normal life, but it had not succeeded as yet."

Cathy put the grimoire down, and looked at the time, how had so much time passed, so quickly. Adam called for Cathy at 6.00pm sharp. She had spent the afternoon, reading, meditating, and thinking about the vampires and sunlight protection. All she could hear in her mind was '*technology.*'

She climbed into Adam's car; witch flight was not allowed as the vampires home was covered in wards to keep people away. Only by invitation or appointment could anyone get near to their house.

They drove onto the main road, heading over to Holme Valley, and after a couple of miles took a small hidden roadway down toward the lake. As the mansion came into view, Cathy saw the huge gates. Slowly begin to open.

"The wards are as good as ever, the gates only open because we have permission that was granted in advance." Adam told her.

Cathy stared ahead of her, she had always known this house was here, but thought it had been abandoned years ago. The driveway seemed to go on for miles, travelling over a small bridge over the Dove Stone Lake. As they neared the house, she saw the manicured lawns on all sides. Eventually the gothic looking mansion came into view. There were turrets, a clock towers and a huge door. The place was enormous.

"Now that is some house," whispered Cathy. Her stomach flipped and the nerves started.

"Wait till you see inside. I promise you will be ok, After all, it is your ancestors that set all this in place. In fact, they still pay rent to your trust. So, I guess, technically you own the house, and are the landlord of the vampires." Adam grinned, as Cathy realised, he was not joking.

"So, in reality, I am the landlord, just checking that all my property is in order?" she grinned back at Adam, "This place must be worth millions."

After parking the car, Adam helped Cathy out of her side. "Did I tell you that you look amazing tonight, and I am so glad you are mine." He whispered in her ear, as they walked to the arched porch over the door that would not have looked out of place on a cathedral.

Pulling on a metal rod at the side of the door, Adam and Cathy heard a church bell like sound, echoing throughout the hallway, which they could just make out through the stained glass on the door.

A man in his mid-forties arrived at the door, within seconds of them ringing the bell.

"Adam and Miss Catherine, how wonderful to see you both, please follow me through to the lounge," the man said to them, as he led them through the huge doorway.

"Thank you, Cathy this is Albers, the one I chatted to on the phone, earlier." Adam explained.

"Pleased to meet you. What an amazing house and entrance hall. Is that painting on the wall this exact house?" Cathy pointed to a huge oil painting on the wall.

"Yes, that was painted around 1860, Monsieur Tomasz found it in an online auction a few years ago. After it was thoroughly cleaned and restored, it was realised it was Ash Way Towers. A lucky find. This way please." He led them through an oak panelled corridor and into a room the size of a football pitch. Complete with a grand piano in one corner, that looked so tiny.

In front of Cathy stood three of the most handsome men, she had ever set eyes on. Immaculately dressed in dark suits and ties. No fangs on show at all. They were so tall, strong looking and so well presented.

"Miss Catherine, it is our pleasure to meet with you at long last." The tallest took her hand and kissed it.

"Pleased to meet you too." Cathy almost drooled.

"I am Tomasz, this is Fillipe, and this charmer is Dumar. We owe you and your ancestors so much. We thank you from the bottom of our hearts, if we had one," Tomasz laughed the sexiest laugh Cathy had heard. The other two joined in. Cathy felt she was falling under a spell, listening to their soft smooth voices and their laughter.

"Come and sit down, let us catch up on dear old Sally," Dumar led her to the sofa. Cathy followed the three vampires across the room, holding tight to Adams hand for reassurance.

"Good evening, Adam" Fillipe joined in the conversation. "Thank you for arranging for us to meet Cathy at such short notice." Turning to Cathy, he continued, "We appreciate you have not been in your role as Coven leader for long. But we have waited as long as we could before requesting this meeting."

"Thank you for inviting me, this house is incredible." She replied.

All three of them laughed at once, "Cathy," Dumar told her, "This is your house, we are only your tenants."

Each of the brothers had a smooth French accent, but their voices varied in the tone and depth.

"I do not understand what I do, and do not own yet. The inheritance is just that, something run by my solicitors and guardians. I thank you for looking after the place though." Cathy started to relax as she chatted to the three vampires.

Suddenly, there was an almighty stampede of feet.

"What is that noise?" Cathy asked, her nerves starting to tremble.

"That noise is actually my two sons," laughed Dumar. "It is near their rest time, but they wanted desperately to meet with you. We are trying to train them to sleep at night but struggling. Their vampire body clocks are working overtime. They will be in here in a moment……"

As he finished saying moment, the door flew open and the most exquisite two young boys ran into the room.

"Boys, what have I told you about running." Dumar's voice was stern but loving.

"But papa, we wanted to meet Miss Cathy, and Mama told us, we must hurry," the elder of the boys said.

"Where is your mother?" Dumar asked.

"I am here, I am afraid the excitement was too much for them." The voice came from a tall, slim, incredibly beautiful woman. "Miss Catherine, I am Franziska, wife of Dumar. These two rascals are Mikael and Izaak. They were so pleased to hear you were visiting. Now boys, say hello."

Suddenly both boys became shy and hid behind their mother.

"Hi, I am Cathy, which is Mikael, and which is Izaak?" Cathy asked the boy vampires.

"I am Mikael," the eldest boy stepped forward and made a tiny bow to Cathy. "He is Izaak, he is only 6."

"Very pleased to meet you Mikael and Izaak." Cathy smiled at the two small boys; *my they would be heartbreakers when they got older,* she thought to herself.

"Come along boys, you have said hello, I am sure Miss Catherine will be a regular visitor to The Towers. You can ask your questions another time." Franziska laughed. "Time for your rest now."

"Nice to meet you both," Cathy laughed, "We can catch up soon, and I will try to answer your questions."

"Are you really a witch?" Izaak whispered to her.

"Yes," Cathy whispered back. "Rest time, and we will meet again soon."

"Boys, say goodnight," Dumar's voice was a bit stronger.

"Goodnight papa, Miss Cathy, Uncle Fillipe, Uncle Tomasz and Monsieur Adam." The boys chorused together and ran out of the room.

Albers came into the lounge and the boys, and their mother left. "Can I organise an aperitif?"

After everyone had given in their drinks order, Cathy took the plunge and said, "What can I help you with? I have been researching and reading the notes that have been written by my ancestors over the years. Quite enlightening."

"Just like your Grandma, straight to the point." Tomasz laughed. "The food system is working fine; I can show you the setup in the cellar if you would like to see. Actually, you can look around anywhere you like. We all have a section of The Towers each. I am on the left-hand side, and Fillipe is on the right-hand side. Dumar, Franziska and the boys are in the coach house, just past the main house. It is connected by an underground tunnel. This middle section of the house is only used occasionally when we have company, like tonight."

"We are all here, all of the time, but we all have different work that we each do. I collect and sell antiques. Mainly online these days. Modern technology is wonderful, Fillipe is the technology wizard, and Dumar is our financial expert." Tomasz continued.

"Dumar, is in the coach house with the boys," laughed Fillipe. "They are not allowed in the main house very often, other than for lessons. Obviously, they are home schooled. The main reason we wanted to meet up is, well I am near to making a breakthrough with our sunlight problem. I have been working in the laboratory, and with silicon chips. I am sure this would work, with the help of your magic.

"That is fantastic," Adam added, "I know you have been trying for years to find a solution."

"I tried to ask the family grimoire today," said Cathy. "But all I could hear was the word 'technology.' Now I understand what it meant. Well, I will be honest, this is a new experience for me, but I will do my absolute best to help. Can I ask a question, that has been puzzling me?"

"Ask away, questions are always a good sign," laughed Fillipe.

"How have you tested the previous trials. I mean, well if you cannot go out in the sunlight, how do you know they don't work?" she asked them.

"We don't sizzle as soon as we walk outside," Tomasz told her. "We can go outside, but not for long. Our skin tells us, it is time to return inside. So, with previous experiments, such as amulets and bracelets, we headed outside, maybe for a little longer. But nothing has worked for us. It is very disappointing; we have been trying for decades."

Albers, entered the room, carrying the drinks. A large glass of dry white wine for Cathy, a cold orange juice for Adam and three glasses of a deep coloured red wine for the brothers. Cathy did not like to ask what they were drinking.

"Cheers to this new adventure, let us all hope that we can be successful." Tomasz raised his glass towards Cathy and the others joined in. "Here, here."

"I must admit, I am not an expert on technology, but with everything that has happened to me lately, anything is possible." She smiled as she saw the four men, admire her. "*Wait until I tell the girls about these three, well two as one was married,*" she thought.

Albers came back into the room to announce that dinner was being server, so Adam and Cathy, followed the three brothers, into another equally impressive dining room. The table in the middle was identical to the board room table at the mill.

Cathy was equally surprised to see the vampires eating the same delicious food as she and Adam ate. She smiled as she thought of her ancestors introducing them to vegetables and not just raw meat."

"Cathy," Fillipe asked, "would it be possible for you to visit during the day soon. I would like to go through my experiments with you and try to work out what magic was needed. Could you ask Sally if she would make an appearance too. I do miss the old girl."

Dumar let out a great belly laugh. "Do not let her hear you call her an old girl. She can still make Cathy do her magic for her."

Franziska had joined them and sat beside Dumar and laughed along with them. The atmosphere of witches, vampires and a shapeshifter were now on a firm level footing. Cathy knew she had nothing to fear from this family.

"Of course, I would love to see the experiments. Yes, I am sure Gran would love to come and visit. She helps me a great deal with my lessons on learning to be a witch." Cathy agreed.

The evening was a huge success, after the food Fillipe took Cathy on a quick tour of the house, whilst Adam stayed with Dumar and Tomasz to catch up on magical police matters. The brothers were also peacekeepers, that flew over the valley during the nights, checking for any troubles.

Cathy was impressed with the technology workshop and could not wait to get back with her Gran, to see if she could help these incredible men.

Chapter 2

Mabon / Harvest

Cathy got herself organised for the trip to Upper Valley coven, to celebrate the Pagan festival of Mabon, or the harvest festival for the Christian church. She was still in awe of her evening with the vampires. Like her Gran had told her, she was glad she had Adam by her side, those vampires were addictive.

The members of the Green Valley coven were meeting in the boardroom of the Riverside Mill. They all had a picnic bag or freezer bag with them, as the invite had said, bring a plate of food for a "Potluck Lunch."

Whilst waiting for the minibus, Cathy brought everyone up to date on her visit to the vampires. Sally, who was floating behind her, "I told you they are incredible men, and Franziska, what a woman. Model and mother. Don't you think?"

"Oh yes, Gran. You were absolutely correct. By the way, they want us two to go back in the next few days. Fillipe says he might have found a breakthrough and wants out help. He says he needs a little input from us. Will you come back with me in the next few days?" Cathy asked.

"It would be my pleasure." Sally agreed, "how are those two little rascals, Izaak and Mikael?"

"Gorgeous, they whispered to me, they asked if I was a real witch, and if I could help them go outside. Do you think we can help them?" Cathy asked.

"I do hope so, they would contribute so much more to the community of Green Valley. If we could find that missing piece." Sally mused.

"Look, here is the minibus," Kim shouted, "shall we get the party started?"

The coven members and guests collected all their belongings. Uncle John helped Margaret; they were never apart these days.

"See you up there," Sally laughed, as she and Clara Jane disappeared into the ether. Whilst everyone else made their way out to the small coach waiting for them

"I hope you are ok with all the witches on this minibus," Cathy laughed to Adam.

"Well, I am not the only man on board. Your Uncle John seems quite happy these days." Adam replied. "Just look at Harold, surrounded by the youngsters!"

"Yes, he seems to have taken Becki and Inese under his wing, he just adores the new café." Cathy laughed, as her friends and family were all excited to be out on another festival meet.

It was just a short drive to the Upper Valley museum, where the coven had their headquarters. The minibus pulled into the car park, which was unusually empty. Glynis and her coven and friends, all came over to greet them.

"Welcome to the home of the Upper Valley Coven," she told them.

"Thank you for inviting us," Cathy shook hands and was pulled into a tight hug.

"I am afraid it won't be anything like your Summer solstice event. But we hope you do enjoy your time with us," Glynis said.

"Nonsense, it will just be as special," Cathy laughed, as the bus from the Nether Valley coven pulled in behind her coach.

"The car park seems quiet today," Cathy asked Glynis.

"Oh, yes, the Morris Men are here soon. They are on a tour of the area, and always stop in the museum car park for a few dances, and drinks at the pub opposite. Shall we take your belongings inside, and show you around our special place?" Glynis asked. So, she led Cathy and Bronwen, Nether Valleys leader, and the others along the canal the path.

"Are we not going through the museum?" Bronwen asked.

"We are not actually in the museum. The museum was the original engine room of another old textile mill. It was converted into the Museum of the Valleys around the 1960s, by a local benefactor. We are in the old mill too, similar to Riverside Mill, but we are hidden away from prying eyes. This way." Glynis led them a short distance on the canal path, and through a semi hidden door, that looked just like part of an old stone wall.

Once inside the entrance hall, Cathy could see what looked like the stone on the outside, was in fact a window on the inside. They overlooked the picturesque canal. Flowing next to the canal was the river, which both flowed through Green Valley and onwards to Nether Valley.

"How fabulous, this setting is amazing." Cathy said, followed by a lot of agreement from the other guests.

"Follow me, we will go into the long gallery, we have set up some tables for the 'potluck' food." Glynis now led the forty plus guests down a corridor and up a flight of steps. Into a massive room, a table was set up down one side of the gallery, already holding plenty of food and drink. Opposite the table, was a glass window, that overlooked the canal and river.

By the time everyone had put their plates on the tables, it turned out to be a wonderful spread. Tables with starters, main courses, desserts, vegetarian, and gluten free food. On one table stood an old-fashioned tea urn.

"That looks interesting," Becki giggled.

"That is the old tea urn, first used by this coven in the late 1800s. They used it when they had meetings and tea and finger sandwiches. Nowadays, we have our own brew of tea," Glynis laughed.

"Sound fun," Becki said.

"It must be drunk in small glasses only," Glynis told her. "It is very own juniper tea – or in other words our very own brand of gin."

"Oh, my word," Becki gasped, "you make your own gin? You have come a long way from tea and sandwiches." Becki and Inese were intrigued with the idea of making their own gin.

Everyone gathered around, as Glynis asked for a moment of their time.

"Fellow witches, wizards, and guests. Welcome to the home of Upper Valley Coven – the Circle of the Ravenstone Coven. A warm welcome to the Circle of the Dove Stone and the Circle of the Buckton Castle Covens. Our coven was started by one of Cathy's ancestors. Around 1800, Hilda the younger sister of Alice, came here to start the new coven. As did the third sister, Marion started the Nether Valley Coven. Isn't that correct Bronwen?" Glynis asked.

"Very much so, Cathy, that makes us all cousins, with the same ancestors the Buckley tree. Although about five or six times removed." Bronwen confirmed.

Glynis continued, "Today we celebrate Mabon, in the Pagan Wheel of the Year. In Christian terms we are celebrating the Harvest Festival. As the grains that were sown at the Midsummer festivals, we now celebrate the growth and collection of these seeds. Please can we start with two prayers, one to Mabon and one to celebrate the gathered harvest. Everyone bowed their heads in respect as Glynis said the prays for thanksgiving.

"Now, it is time to celebrate," she told the group. "Please make yourselves at home, grab a drink and enjoy the view. Remember, the juniper tea is on tap, but take it slowly."

"Thank you so much," Cathy and Bronwen said.

"We have the Morris Men outside at 4.00pm. Until then we can relax and enjoy. Phew," Glynis relaxed. "I was so nervous about that."

"Why so nervous?" asked Bronwen.

"I have never welcomed anyone other than my own coven before. Like you two, I am still new to being the leader of the coven." Glynis told them.

"I know just what you mean," laughed Bronwen.

"Hey, Gran," called Cathy, to the ghost of her Grandma. "Care to explain, how the three of us are all new together?"

"Not much to explain Catherine. We are three extremely proud grandmothers, proud of our three granddaughters. Your stories are all similar, sent away at a young age, for you to eventually take your rightful place." Sally laughed.

Sofia was next, "Bronwen, you have followed my footsteps at Nether Valley. You were my rightful successor. We were lucky as we did get to spend time together before I left the mortal earth."

"Likewise," Sarah joined in. "Glynis, you too were in training with me. But the three of you will achieve great success, if you all work together. It is so wonderful for us three ghostly Grandmas, to see you all getting on so well."

"Wow," the three younger witches stood in awe, as the three older ghosts smiled at them.

They soon realised the room had gone quiet. They looked to see everyone stood staring at the three ghosts.

"Welcome ladies, so good to see the three of you together again." Harold smiled. "It is because Catherine is here today, that we are all able to see you."

Cathy checked Glynis and Bronwen, who both were almost in tears. This was the first time they had seen the ghosts of the dearly departed Grandmas.

"Will we still be able to see you when Cathy leaves?" Bronwen asked her Grandma.

"Yes, my dear. Your powers, along with this full room of witches, has enabled Sarah and me to return." Sofia told her.

"Why didn't this happen at Midsummer?" Cathy asked Sally.

"We were outside, there was not enough concentrated power. But since then, you have grown more into your powers, and in this space today, magic happens." Sally told them. Glynis and Bronwen walked to their respective ancestors.

Cheers went up in the room, as the reunion took place.

When everything settled back into drinking and eating, and generally having a good time, Cathy slipped her arm into Sally's. "Thank you, Gran," she whispered.

"Catherine, when will you realise your own ability. This is your own doing, not mine." Sally smiled at the young woman in her arms.

4.00pm arrived and Glynis led the group, down a small staircase and into the actual museum.

"We don't want the crowds to see the coven entrance, and forty plus people on the canal tow path may cause a stir. So, we use this route."

"I understand. It is years since I have visited the museum. I most come back soon," replied Cathy.

"We can have a short tour later when the public have gone. One of our coven members, actually is an assistant to the curator." Glynis told her. "Sometimes it gets a little spooky after hours. I am excited to see what affect you have on the place."

"Now you have me worried," Cathy giggled. She felt so happy to be out and about with her now long-lost cousins, and her coven family.

"You have nothing to worry about Cathy, accept the gifts you have been given. Adam here will look after you," Glynis laughed as she nudged Adam in the ribs.

"She is correct Cathy, you have your powers, accept, and use them. If magic fails, I will be here for you." Adam teased her, "Now let's go see the dancing."

Crowds stood around, what was once an empty car park. Not only were the Valley's Morris men there, but about ten other groups. Some dressed in the white shirts, multicoloured waistcoats, black pants, and clogs. Along with the famous hat with flowers all over. Others dressed in all black outfits, lady dancers in traditional dress. It all made for a very colourful view.

The ladies were dancing first, the sound of drums and accordions filled the valley.

The dancing and merriment went on for a few hours. A couple of trips across to the pub, kept the Morris Men's glasses refilled, and the crowd itself drank a fair amount.

Eventually the Morris Men led the procession further along the high street, to finish off their evening in 'the square,' at the centre of Upper Valley.

"I really enjoyed that," Adam told Cathy, as they made their way back inside the museum. "I didn't think it would be my sort of thing, but it looks like hard work to me. All that dancing, walking, and drinking,"

Cathy laughed with him and told him to look over at Becki and Inese, chatting to a couple of the young Morris men. "Looks like they have enjoyed it too."

When they all got back inside, Becki and Inese came to Cathy and whispered they had a date the week after. "Weren't they amazing?" Inese gushed.

Cathy and Adam smiled at the two women, not that much younger than themselves, both appeared love struck – or was it the juniper tea?

"They were all amazing, the work they put into those dances, it makes me breathless. But we can have a sneak preview in the museum later – how fun will that be?" Cathy told them.

"Scary," they both laughed, and headed back towards the tea urn queue.

The evening wore on, Cathy keeping an eye on her younger members. Around 10.00pm, Glynis invited anyone that wanted, to join her to have a quick tour of the museum.

Not everyone wanted to go around an old museum after dark, so they stayed to dance the night away, with the same DJ, that led the music at the midsummer party.

Glynis led those wanting to see the old artefacts, through a small door, just off the entrance to the main room. A middle-aged woman got a set of keys from her handbag and opened the small door.

When Cathy walked through the door, she could feel the atmosphere in the museum. The smell of old exhibits made her nose twitch.

"Do you think we will feel anything in here tonight?" Gillian asked Cathy.

"I hope not, it would be nice to have a night off witchy stuff." Cathy answered.

They walked into the first exhibition room, Cathy studied the reconstruction of the three valleys, over the millennia. Starting with the prehistoric times through to the industrial revolution. How the houses in the tiny hamlets on the hillsides, moved into the valleys, to be near the river.

The second room had a recreated small house, that would have been found on the hillside. A working weavers cottage. All one small room, with a bed on a pulley system so it could be lowered when needed. Cathy thought to herself, *"how many people lived in this small cottage, and animals too?"*

Cathy could have spent hours in the museum, and she knew she would revisit soon. She had felt something when she had stood near the old cottage but wasn't sure what it was. She followed the others through the museum, stopping and reading the dates and imagining her own ancestors in situ.

Every new exhibition hall showed the group more and more history of the valleys. Cathy whispered to Adam, that they must come back soon, and take more time. She felt she needed to relearn all her family history.

When the tour ended Cathy breathed out, causing Adam to laugh. "Did you get away with any ghostly feelings?"

"I think so, there was definitely something in the old weavers cottage, I would like to come back to. Otherwise, we went around pretty quick, so no one had chance to get to me." Cathy giggled. "There were one or two cold spots that I feel need to be investigated, at a later date, and not with a group of people."

Making their way back to the main room, Cathy noticed the whole room was up dancing, and Becki and Inese seemed to be leading a variation on the conga dance. Joining in, the evening sped by too quickly, and soon it was time to leave.

"We will all meet up again soon, at our headquarters. We are in the old town hall, totally different from both the museum and the mill." Bronwen reminded them.

"Sounds good to me, cousin," Cathy and Glynis both said at the same time.

"We need an evening researching our ancestry, to see how many generations there actually are, in our blood line," Suggested Cathy.

"Again, another good idea," laughed the other two.

As they all made their way back along the canal side tow path, Cathy caught a glimpse of two men, dressed in what looked like old navigators clothing.

"Who are they?" she pointed them out to Glynis.

"I have no idea, I have never seen them before, ghosts maybe, that have heard of you?" she giggled.

"I think you are correct," Adam said, "I can only make out an outline of two figures."

"Shall I go and talk to them?" Cathy asked.

"I think we should ask Peter, if he has done any archaeology on the canal, then you can work out what they want." Adam replied.

"To think, I thought I had an evening off," Cathy smiled, s she waved to the two men watching her. She sent them a telepathic message to say she would be back, at which they both made a small bow and nodded. *They got the message,* she thought to herself.

"We best get this lot back home," Adam motioned towards the Green Valley members, "some look a little worse for wear."

As the minibus meandered back to the mill, dropping people off at their own homes, everyone thanked Cathy for making the coven a joyous group again.

"I think you did good today, Cathy," Adam said when he helped her off the bus.

"I have really enjoyed it, finding out that we are all somehow related. But now I have two more ghosts to try to help." Cathy sighed.

"I will text Peter in the morning, you get some rest, aren't you back with the vampires tomorrow?" and with that, he saw she was already fast asleep.

Chapter 3

The Vampire's Lab

Cathy awoke and wondered where she was, then realised she was at Adams. "How did I get here? I remember arriving back at the mill last night."

Adam laughed, "You fell asleep as soon as we got back, so I used witch flight to get us back here."

"Oh, yes, the day at Upper Valley. That was a good day. Oh My, I have got to get ready for the meeting with the vampires." Cathy sat up, too quickly. "My what was in that juniper tea?"

"Gin, that is what was in the tea, how much did you have?" Adam snorted.

"I best have a long shower and try to sober up." Cathy kissed Adam as she moved to the bathroom.

Before long, she was on her way, in her old dependable mini, to the vampires home. Even though Cathy could now afford a new car, she just felt it wasn't viable, as she didn't use her own car very much. Witch flight covered a lot of miles.

Driving over the Holme Valley Road, Cathy admired the view of the green hills in front of her. She just hoped the gates would open for her again. It felt very weird that she had actually inherited all that she had, including this magnificent mansion.

Cathy turned off the main road, she saw the tall metal gates slowly begin to open. She put the car in first gear and slowly drove down the lane, admiring the view. Her visit with Adam, had been at night, so the view had been hidden. The grounds looked like they had been manicured with tiny scissors. Trees shaped into various animals; "*someone is good at topiary,*" She thought to herself.

Parking in the same spot as she had before, Cathy climbed out of her small red mini, stretching herself, and smoothing her casual clothes. The black dress from her previous meeting, was safely stored away, back in the wardrobe.

Sally was waiting for her by the side of the arched door. "Hi darling, I would never miss an opportunity to meet with these boys," she said to her. Cathy wondered about her Grandma at times.

"Hi Gran, I am glad you are here with me, you were totally right about the trio."

Cathy rang the church-like bell, soon she saw Albers walking across the entrance hall.

"Is Albers a vampire?" Cathy whispered.

"Oh no, he is a wizard, a very old wizard," Sally grinned as she whispered back to Cathy, and the door slowly opened.

Albers fully opened the huge oak door, and almost flung himself at Sally, but luckily, he remembered that she was a ghost. "Oh, my darling Sally. It is so wonderful to see you again. What a marvellous granddaughter you have Sally. The ability to bring you back to us. Please come inside."

"Master Fillipe is in his workshop; I will take you directly to him. The other brothers will join us for lunch later." Albers led them through a few corridors, towards the back of the building, until they arrived at the usual small hidden door.

"Gran?" Cathy asked, "Is the house built in the same style as the mill, secret doors and long corridors, even the same table as the mill's board room table."

"Yes, it is all the same magic, my dear." Sally confirmed.

On hearing voices, Fillipe came to the small door and opened it to let in his visitors. "Welcome, please come through. Sally, a pleasure to be able to see you again. Cathy, always a pleasure," he said bending to kiss her hand.

"*This man could be addictive*," thought Cathy.

"This room is very much like my Temple Room, back at the mill, but with so much more technology." Cathy counted at least six computer screens, all running a series of data on them.

"Ladies, please come inside, let me update you on my latest experiments." Fillipe showed them towards a desk set with extra chairs next to it.

Cathy walked through the space between the rows of desks and workspaces. She felt the same as she did in her own Temple Room, the feeling of peace and protection.

Soon they were all stood in front of a large computer screen, latest technology that one would expect. "Let me show you my, shall we say, the prototype." Fillipe said.

"Fillipe, you have been busy, since I was last here," Sally said, almost flirting with the vampire.

"Ahh, Sally, you know me so well, I am always trying to find the missing link to our sunlight problem. I work constantly on this." Fillipe sighed.

"Tell me what you are working on?" Cathy asked, tentatively. She was unsure how she was going to help the vampires walk in the sunlight.

"Well, where do I start. We have tried amulets, bracelets, waistcoats, all with different chemicals and magic. Nothing has ever worked. We have tried so many experiments over the years. This latest attempt is using every new technology there is available. I am working with silicon chips, something that could be like an implant. But it is missing something." Fillipe showed them some pictures on the computer screen.

"This is a prototype. The magnification will show you the workings, see here…" Fillipe zoomed in on the screen. Showing them a complicated microchip."

"What does that do?" Cathy asked.

"I have put in all the information, that has been compiled over the decades. The night temperature and daytime temperatures. How body clocks work, compared to human body clocks – gained with Sally's help, many years ago. We have coordinated so many pieces of information over the years. But I just feel we just need some of you magic, and a missing link. Something, I just can't put my finger on." Fillipe struggled to say.

Cathy immediately knew how important this was to the vampires. She hadn't given it that much serious thought. It hit her, that she was the one they were relying on now.

"Gran, what magic do I need to do, and how can we find the missing link?" Cathy asked.

"The grimoire will help you with the necessary magic. It always showed me what it thought we needed. But this missing piece, if only we all knew. But something tells me, you will find it, sooner rather than later." Sally told her granddaughter.

"No pressure then," Cathy laughed, trying to ease the situation.

"Catherine. There is no pressure, we have been working on this for many a decade, with quite a few of your ancestors. We are patient, but we will keep trying." Fillipe reassured her. "Now, I think it is time for us to go and join the others, for some lunch."

Joining the other vampires, in the large dining room, Cathy relaxed for a while, and tried to put this new quest to the back of her mind for a while. Waiting for them was Tomasz, alongside Dumar and his family. The two young vampires looked like they had been told to be on best behaviour. Cathy sat next to young Izaak, who turned to smile at her.

"Can you help us, Miss Cathy?" he whispered. "I so want to play football outside in the daylight."

Cathy's heart broke, to feel that the people she was sat with, had never had the pleasure of sitting outside in the sunshine, to feel the warmth of the sun, or even the coldness of the snow. They had only ever been outside in the darkness.

"Yes, Izaak, I will be able to help you. Somehow." Cathy promised. *"Or I hope I can,"* she thought to herself.

Chapter 4

Tamara and Barney

Cathy was still excited about her meeting with the vampires again, and her mind was working overtime. Since the meeting with Fillipe, in his workshop, her mind had been working overtime.

She had read and read over again her grimoire. In her own Temple Room, Cathy had spent hours looking at the past spells her ancestors had tried. When she meditated, holding the grimoire in her arms, she just saw pictures of the sun and moon, but put that down to the reason behind the research. She had the words in her mind for the spell work, but she still felt something was off.

She looked at her watch and realised she had promised to meet Adam at the café, and to update him on her work. So, she left the spell work for the time being. Walking through the complex maze of corridors from her apartment to the café, Cathy was smiling to herself at the new buzz of activity.

Now that it was early in the Santa Season, suddenly the delivery vans were queueing up on the top yard. The old warehouse now had the large roller shutter door open, and a huge truck and container were being unloaded. Cathy smiled to herself, now I guess the Christmas Grotto well underway.

The café was now so popular, that Cathy had her own table behind the counter, so not to take up paying customer seats. She was looking at the menu, even though she knew just what she would be ordering. Her magic intuition told her Adam was on his way. She looked up to see him just as he entered the café. *"He is so perfect,"* she thought to herself. After the disaster of her first marriage, Cathy had thought she would never find someone to love, so soon. Especially now she had learnt that she was a witch.

"Morning Cathy," Adam took his seat beside her, landing a kiss on her cheek as he sat down.

"How are things in Santa Ville?" he teased.

"I absolutely love it," Cathy laughed. Christmas had always been her favourite time of year. A time when her Uncle John had pulled all stopes out and the photo albums of her late parents. The time was special for them to reminisce about them. He had looked after her so well.

"How are the Magical Police?" Cathy asked, knowing full well, he wouldn't tell her anything, with everything being confidential.

"Pretty boring, to be honest. Can't you get a new quest or adventure to gives us some work?" he laughed back.

"I have the vampire spell to create, but that's the only quest I want at the moment. Let me enjoy all the Christmas activities. Even though, I have to attend the Opening of the Portal soon. That scares me a bit." Cathy told him.

"Orders please," Becki interrupted them and laughed. "Or is it just the usual for you both?"

"Usual for me," Cathy answered laughing, "Same Adam? Busy day again Becki? You two opened up just in time."

"Cathy, it is fantastic, the delivery drivers are all regulars already, some say they will be back at weekend with their families too. We wouldn't be here without your help. Thank you again." Becki beamed as she looked around the packed café.

"Huge success I would say," Stephen, Adam's grandfather said, as he came around the corner to join them. "You might need to extend around here for the regulars if it carries on like this."

The trio sat and chatted about everyday life, as they drank their coffee and ate their lunches.

They all turned as they heard a commotion in the main café area. A worried Becki came over to Adam to tell him someone was asking for him.

"There is a woman asking for you, and she said she had been told she would find you here. Err, she says she is your wife." A terrified Becki told them.

Cathy choked on her coffee when Adam stood up to leave.

"This shouldn't take long," he reassured her.

"That woman is nothing but a trouble causer," Stephen told Cathy. "She married my eldest grandson, because she thought he was rich, with us being an old established family in the area. We do live rather comfortably, for sure, but she was never actually in love with him. He was just a steppingstone for her to get the life she thought she actually wanted. Too much like your ex-husband, I am sorry to add. I better go and see what she wants now."

He too stood up to leave, so Cathy followed too. They walked into the main area of the café, and Cathy saw Adam talking to a tall blonde woman, he had hold of her elbow and was leading her towards the doorway. Following them was a young boy, Cathy thought he looked around the age of five or six.

"Is that the ex-wife?" she asked Stephen.

"Yes, it is her, but I have no idea who the child is. She and Adam didn't have any children. She always said she had a problem conceiving, or something. Personally, I don't think children were in her plans." Harold scoffed. It was obvious to Cathy he didn't like the woman.

"I think we would be best staying inside Cathy; it looks a bit heated outside." Stephen led her back to the table they had just left.

Cathy felt dizzy and sick, and Becki noticed she didn't look well.

"Are you alright Cathy?" Becki came over and asked her. "You look like you just seen the devil."

"I think I have, Becki," Cathy whispered, "My mind is working overtime. But I am getting some serious bad vibes. I think I will go back to the apartment and have a chat with my gran. Stephen, Will you tell Adam were I have gone."

Cathy left the café by the back door, that led straight into the corridor of the mill. A quick exit was what she needed, something felt seriously off. She made her way back to the apartment and summoned her Grandma right away.

"What on earth is the matter?" Sally asked, she too could feel something was seriously wrong.

"Let me get inside the apartment Gran, I need to be alone with you." Cathy went into the lounge of the apartment, collapsed on the huge sofa, and broke her heart.

"Cathy, what is it?" her worried Gran asked.

"Adam's ex-wife arrived at the café." She wept.

"I am sure, It is nothing my dear." Sally comforted her.

"I had a premonition Gran. She arrived, and then Adam took them our into the yard. There was a young child with her. My premonition or gut instinct is that the child is Adams. So, he will do the correct thing, and she will move back in with him. How do I stop it Gran, my heart is breaking." Cathy asked. Sally hugged her granddaughter the best she could being a ghost. "Oh, my poor child, I feel it too. But nothing you can say or do will help. Adam is a good man, and genuinely loves you. But, as you said, we know he will take on his responsibilities. All you can do is bide your time. She will slip up eventually. I genuinely don't believe she has a child with Adam, because she would have asked for money before now, not wait for years."

"But Gran, I feel so helpless. Maybe I am wrong." Cathy tearfully tried to hope she had been wrong in her premonition.

Clara Jane appeared after hearing the crying. "What is happening, Oh Miss Cathy why are you so upset?"

Sweet Clara Jane, murdered in 1884, and still haunting the old mill. Sally updated Clara Jane about Adam's ex-wife. Gillian too came in from the retail shop next door to the apartment. Becki had rung her to explain what had happened.

Gillian got some strong coffee. Oskar, and Marley, the two familiars, snuggled close to Cathy to take some of her worries away from her. The whole room felt the unease that Adam's ex-wife had brought with her.

'Ping' Cathy checked her phone. Sure, enough it was a text from Adam. *'we need to talk.'* Was all it said.

She looked around the group of witches, ghosts and familiars that had gathered around her. "What do I reply?" she asked them.

Sally was the one to take the lead and answer her.

"Text him, do what you need to do – I already know." Sally told her.

Very nervously, Cathy felling like her world was ending, replied as her Gran had told her.

"Do what you need to do. I already know what you have to tell me. But please be careful Adam," and she pressed send, as her heart broke a little more.

Immediately a reply came through. *"How do you know?"*

"Witch's intuition. I will magic my belongings from the house immediately, take care Adam."

Cathy stared at the people she loved more than anything in the world, and finally sobbed her heart out.

Clara Jane and Sally disappeared to Adam's house and along with Gillian doing Witch-flight, they magically moved all Cathy's belongings. Not that there was much to move, being a witch, the wardrobe was magicked, as necessary.

Gillian took back what she could and left the two ghosts to finish off. They made themselves invisible, as they saw Adam and his ex-wife arrive back at the house.

"Barney, go upstairs and choose a bedroom, whilst I talk to your father." Tamara told him. "Do as you are told," she shouted at the boy, who was stood motionless, looking at the man, this woman had just called his father.

"Poor child," Clara Jane whispered to Sally.

"But I don't understand, Tamara, we didn't have any children, you never wanted them." Adam, like Cathy, looked like his world had ended.

"I was pregnant when I left you. I had the child, but my sister looked after him for me. I had met and married Bob and went to live in the USA. But I have missed my son so much, that I have come back to get him, and bring him back to his daddy." Tamara smugly told Adam. "Bob never got over the fact that I had a child, so we are now divorced. Mel, my sister, told me that I should tell you about Barney and how we should be a family all together. You haven't met anyone, have you?"

"What are you talking about, Tamara, We didn't have a child. What is it to you if I am in a relationship?" Adam raised his voice.

"Oh, I had heard a rumour you had set up house with a rich bitch and you were spending her inheritance. But this house hasn't changed one bit since I left, so I doubt you got s new friend. But it is ideal for me and the boy to move back into." Tamara told him, as she made herself at home.

Adam was dumbstruck, when he had gone to work this morning, the house was full of Cathy and her things. Now it was bare, "*How did she know?*" he thought to himself.

"I am not sure what to say, Tamara." Adam tried to catch her up as she was walking around the house, inspecting everything. "Tell me more about Barney."

Sally and Clara Jane had heard too much. Everything Cathy had felt, was really happening. Cathy needed them now. Out of the corner of his eye, Adam spied Sally, just as she vanished, but he could tell, she had heard everything that had been said.

Looking around, he saw the small boy sat on the stairs, and went over to him. "Hi Barney, want to tell me about yourself, over some snacks and a drink?"

"Please," the small boy seemed petrified by the whole situation. Adam led him to the kitchen and got some bits from the pantry. He knew he couldn't use his magic in front of strangers.

Tamara came marching in, after giving herself a tour of the house, and satisfied no one had moved in. "Coffee for me," she ordered. "The removal van is booked for morning. We shall be back to normal in a day or two. Come here Barney, shall we get to know your Daddy."

Back at the apartment, in the mill. Sally had told Cathy that her premonition was 100% accurate. "What is she playing at? But I do know that boy isn't her son. He looked scared to death."

Gillian, always one to take your mind of things, "Cathy, why don't you do a bit of researching, and find the birth certificate? We could try to find out to whom the boy actually belongs."

"Maybe in a day or two. I just want to go to sleep. Gran, can you recommend a good sleeping spell to last a few days, please." Cathy muttered. "I am sorry everyone, but can I please ask to be left alone for a while. I know you are all here for me, but I just want to curl up and sleep – and forget all about men for a while."

Everyone left the room, or faded into thin air, and Cathy found herself alone. Glancing at her phone, she saw missed calls and text messages. She switched the power off on her phone and went to crawl into her own bed. She knew in her heart Adam was her man, but she just didn't know how to get through the next part of her life, without him.

Chapter 5

Who is Barney?

Cathy woke from her restless sleep, hoping everything was just a distant dream. Slowly she crawled from her bed, trying to avoid Oskar. He had guarded her throughout the night and daytime, as she slept. He thought that if his mistress was in shock and pain, then so was he.

As Cathy stumbled into her kitchen, Clara Jane and Sally were waiting quietly for her.

"Morning Cathy, I assume you didn't sleep well?" her Grandma asked her.

"I took a sleeping tablet about 2.00am. That knocked me out for a while," Cathy told them.

"Have you checked your phone this morning?" an agitated Clara Jane asked.

"No, I switched it off, why?" Cathy relied, wondering what the young ghost was up to now.

"Oh," she said sheepishly, "well I just happened to be floating past Adam' house. He didn't look happy and kept checking his phone. Her ladyship was upstairs with the boy. Poor child, he looks so frightened of her. I think Adam was hoping to speak to him, alone, but she doesn't let them be alone together."

Cathy got up and went to collect her mobile, from her bedroom. Oskar was staring at her, with a look of concern on his face.

"How are you feeling Cathy?" he asked. "You must have cried most of the night, I felt helpless, I wish I could help you more."

"We will be OK. Gran and Clara Jane are in the kitchen, shall we go back in there." Cathy stroked his bushy ginger fur. *"Would she be alright though,"* she thought to herself. *"She had let her guard down and fallen in love with Adam, she couldn't go through the heartbreak she felt after her first husband left her."*

As she walked back down the corridor to the kitchen, Cathy pressed the on switch for her mobile phone. Immediately, the buzz of incoming messages filled the silence.

"Well, Clara Jane." Cathy said, "You were right, he has sent a lot of messages. I think I need a strong coffee whilst I work my way through them all. I have nothing to hid from any of you, and I will admit, I feel so raw and desolate at the moment." She clicked her fingers and her favourite mug, full of strong coffee appeared in front of her.

"What does he say?" Clara Jane hovered near to Cathy, trying to see the phone screen.

"They are all basically the same," Cathy told her. "Cathy, answer me, Are you there, It must be a mistake, Cathy call me, please. The messages are all like that, but lots of them."

"Oh Gran, what shall I do. I feel so unsure. Part of me hates myself because I cannot handle these situations. But until I find out for sure, I have to watch my soul partner live with someone else." Cathy leaned toward her Grandma, who could feel the pain herself.

Sally thought back, when she had heard that Harold had died in the war, her life finished. Walter helped her get back to some sort of normal life, but part of her had died with Harold. When he came back, life was so different for them all. She didn't want Cathy to make any rash decisions like she had done.

Cathy continued, "I lost my Mum and Dad, I was used by my first husband, I don't think I can cope with Adam being snatched away too."

"Cathy, my love, we all need you to be strong. If anyone can solve this – it is you. Now, go and shower and put some decent clothes on. We need to check out this woman. But first of all, message Adam. Tell him you are all right, under the circumstances, you don't want him worrying about you and the current problems. We don't want either of you being ill. Tell him to take his time, but that you are working on the matter too. We all feel that this woman is not telling the truth, but we don't know what her game is. Personally, if she had had a child with Adam, she would have been after money before now. I will go and ask Harold, to check in with Brian, his dad, to see if the Magical Police can throw any light on her recent movements."

"Yes Gran," Cathy said, straightening up. "you are so right, there is no point me wallowing in pity, when an imposter is in our ranks."

"You two are soul mates, just look at his surname," Sally giggled.

"Why do you say that gran?" Cathy asked.

"Well, he is called Buckley, our ancestors run side by side. When you two are married – you will be Cathy Buckley, following the rest of your ancestors!"

"Wow, I had never thought of that, that's scary Gran. Talking about marriage when his ex-wife and son are with him."

"You will be fine, eventually. This is just a test for how strong your love is. Now, go and text him back, put him out of his misery, then shower and change. Then it's time for you to hit the genealogy sites. Like Clara Jane suggested last night, try to find the birth certificate of the boy. We heard he was called Barney, so should be simple – to rule him out as Adam's son." Sally pushed her towards the bedroom. "Get your working head on, you will need it."

Thirty minutes later, showered, dressed and the text message sent. Cathy took her place at her laptop.

"Right, let's go to work on this woman, and who the poor boy is. Sadly, I never asked Adam about his ex, we just put of them in a box, and threw the key away." Cathy said wishfully.

"Try the marriage certificate first, the one to Adam, that will tell you her maiden name," Clara Jane suggested. She had got into genealogy, when she spent a lot of time with her relative, Cynthia – who was in fact her 2 x great niece!

"That's a good place to start. Clara Jane, you are a star. What a great idea, I am so lucky to have you with me." Cathy started the search, she had a vague idea on the year, as it was similar dates to her own first marriage.

The computer search engines whizzed as Cathy went to work. "Look, here it is, that was quick." Cathy exclaimed. "Geez, they married the exact same week as Martin, and I married. Look Adam John Buckley married Tamara Nugent."

"That's a bit scary, looks like the fates got things a bit mixed up. Both couples would have been better off with the other's partner." Giggled Sally. "Or was it a lesson for you both? Who knows."

"Tamara Nugent, daughter of Arthur Nugent, from Upper Valley, well she is from a local family then. The witnesses are here too, Melanie Nugent, that's got to be her sister. The other witness is Rob Buckley, that's Adam's younger brother, who we met at the cabin."

Cathy was slowly forgetting her worries, as the genealogy searching was taking her mind away from her own troubles to a whole new investigation. Searching for peoples background and family came natural to Cathy, although she didn't really do modern day searching, usually historical.

"I will check the electoral rolls for the Nugent family of Upper Valley. There can't be many Nugent's around." Cathy even sounded brighter, and Sally and Clara Jane smiled at each other, knowingly.

"How about looking for a marriage for Melanie Nugent," Oskar joined the conversation, "the child might be her sisters."

Over the next few hours, Cathy, her ghosts, and familiars searched every website and idea that they could come up with. They were trying to piece together, every scrap of information they could find, to work out what Tamara was up to.

"Cathy," Oskar whispered to her, "why don't you text Adam and ask him her family details, he should know the family, and save you some time searching."

"I don't know, he hasn't replied to my earlier text yet," Cathy's mask slipped off her face, as she thought of Adam.

"I understand it is difficult Cathy, but I am sure he wants all this sorting out, just as quick as you do." Sally reassured her.

Just as they were talking, Gillian came down the corridor from the crystal shop.

"Cathy, there is someone to see you in the shop. Yes, it is Adam, and quite frankly, he looks as rough as you do," Gillian told her.

"I don't think I can see him just yet," Cathy stumbled over her words. Her stomach flipped inside.

"Go and see him, in private. Take him into the Temple Room." Sally suggested.

"He has never been allowed in there, Maybe this is the reason why." Cathy told her.

"Catherine, go now, or you may live to regret your decision," Sally argued.

Cathy magically checked that she looked ok and followed Gillian back down the corridors to the retail shop unit. As she entered the shop area, Adam flung himself at her and nearly knocked her off her feet.

"Not here Adam, follow me through here," and Cathy led him back down the short corridors. As she neared the Temple Room, she turned to Adam. "This will be a test, if the Temple Room lets you in, after all this time. If it does, I know we will be ok."

"I do hope so." Muttered Adam in his reply.

Before Cath could put her hand on the door handle, the door opened itself, to let them both cross the threshold.

"That's a first, and a good sign," Cathy tried to joke.

"Cathy," Adam was nearly crying. "I don't know where to begin. Tamara claims that she was pregnant when we split up, but her sister raised the boy. She went to live in America with her new husband. But I don't believe her, why wouldn't she tell me that we had a son, before now. I just don't know what game she is playing. She would have claimed maintenance off me, that's for certain. Or, knowing Tamara, she wouldn't have kept the baby. She was so against getting pregnant, it would have spoilt all her cunning plans."

The pair hugged, as if they had no tomorrow. "Cathy, what can we do, I cannot turn my back on a small child. I have asked her to do a blood test, or a DNA test, but she went berserk, and called me all sorts of names, saying I didn't trust her. But I don't!"

Cathy brought Adam up to speed on the research they had done so far. "Do you think, Barney could actually be her sister's child?"

"I have no idea; I haven't seen her since the wedding. I wouldn't know her if I walked past her in the street. She tried to get her claws into our Rob, but he knew straight away the family was bad news.

"Where is Rob playing now?" Cathy asked, she had met the younger guitar playing brother just the once.

"He is in Germany at the moment, but back off to Texas, to catch up with Liv in a couple of weeks. They are both hoping to get over here for Christmas, that will be good. I hope." Adam glad for a break in the Tamara conversation.

"Cathy, please remember, what happens in the future, I love you and you are my soul mate. Just know I would never leave you. This is just a hiccup from a very bitter woman. I think she has been spying on me, as she asked if I was still seeing the rich bitch, that owned most of the area. I told her I wasn't seeing anyone, to keep her off your back, I am sure she is after money." Adam poured his heart out to Cathy, and the Temple Room flickered it's lights in agreement.

"This room is amazing by the way," Adam smiled, "Thank you for letting me in, I hope I am able to return, under better circumstances."

Again, the lights flickered. Cathy laughed. "Even the Temple Room knows and is on our side."

"Soul mate, shall we join the others, and get some more researching done." Cathy smiled as Adam planted a kiss on her lips.

Hand in hand they went back into the kitchen where the group of ghosts had been joined by Becki and Inese and their laptops.

"Come on everyone, we have work to do. Adam asked for a DNA test to prove that Barney is his son, but she refused. So that tells its own story. We need to find out who this boy really belongs too, and what her game is. But, in the meantime, we have to let her think that we know nothing about what she is trying to do." Cathy told the assembled bunch.

Sally smiled as her granddaughter and Adam stood together. She never had any doubts, but time would heal the pair. In her lifetime Sally had known true love only came around once in a lifetime. She counted herself lucky, to have a second chance with Harold, even if it was in her afterlife.

"Adam, tell us what you know about Tamara and her family. We have found a Melanie Nugent, on your marriage certificate as a witness. Do you think that young Barney, could actually be her child?" Sally asked the same question, that Cathy had pondered.

"Do I think that Barney is of my own blood?" Adam spoke quietly. "I just don't know. He is a fabulous little chap but scared to speak in front of Tamara. Yet, she tries her best not to leave us alone. I can say one thing, I do not feel to have any chemistry with him, as a blood relative would."

Cathy let out a sigh of relief, "Do you think we should try and contact this sister?"

"Let's just leave that for now, we need to find out more about her." Sally said.

"I think I had better get back before she gets any ideas. I haven't told her about Cathy and myself – you did a good job of removing Cathy from the house. I will try and ask her how her sister is doing and will gauge her reaction and text you." Adam stood to take his leave.

"We will be ok," Cathy told him as she walked back through to the shop door with him.

"I love you Cathy, Please always remember," Adam kissed her and then left.

Cathy went back to the apartment kitchen, with a renewed vigour.

"Right, back to work, have we found anything yet?" She asked.

"Yes," Becki shouted, "Melanie Nugent married a few months after Adam and Tamara. To a chap called Bob Walker, at the local registry office. There is also a birth record for a birth of a son, around the same age as Barney. We are just running a search through social media."

"Well done, you two are superstars." Cathy smiled. "So, we have Melanie Nugent, marrying Bob Walker and they have a young son. I wonder if social media would let us see any pics of the family?"

Inese spoke up, "Cathy I am checking Instagram and found a Mel Walker, but it is a private profile, so we can't see anything. Let me try Facebook."

"Do we know Tamara's latest surname? We heard she remarried after her divorce from Adam?" Becki asked.

"To be honest, I have no idea. I will text Adam to see if he knows the name of her second husband," Cathy reached for her phone and typed out a text message. "That should save some searching time."

"Yippee." Whooped Inese. "Facebook has the sister on a public profile."

Everyone crowded around Inese and the very public Facebook page of a couple enjoying what looked like an amazing holiday. "Looks like they are on a cruise, and in the Caribbean." Becki said. "Have they won the lottery?"

"Something isn't right on this profile and the photos. Where is their son?" Cathy asked. "The photos have no child in them, where is he?"

Cathy's phone beeped with an incoming message. *'Bill McIlroy – second husband.'*

A further message came through, *'Tamara remarried last year, not seen sister for years as she moved down south. They met up at an arranged place to hand over Barney, she says!!'*

'Thanks, sister is on a Caribbean cruise according to Facebook.' Cathy replied

"Where is her second husband. I do hope he isn't in the USA, like Annie Bradley." Clara Jane asked the group.

"Oh No. I hadn't thought of that. I will message Brian for him to check it out with the Magical Police Agency." Cathy pondered. "I think I have had enough for today, my head aches. I need a bit more sleep, and to try to forget that woman living in Adam's house."

Sally looked at her granddaughter. "We will keep looking quietly, while you go and relax, sleep, meditate, switch off your mind, if you can. I will ask Brian to make the enquiries."

"We will go back up to the café, we will let Kim and Wendy know where we are up to, so they can put fresh eyes on the case. We will all keep searching for answers for you Cathy," Becki told her.

"We love you so much Cathy, you are like our older sister, and we are all one family." Inese told her as they left the apartment.

Sally, Clara Jane, and Oskar told her they would be in the kitchen, and Harold was joining them too, if she needed anything.

"We need to wrap this up with this imposter," growled Oskar, "I don't like Catherine being upset."

"Let's leave her alone for a while. I will hover in the background. Clara Jane, could you go and bring Donna Maria up to date please." Sally asked the young ghost. Harold and Sally sat in silence in Cathy's kitchen, both deep in thought.

Oskar stalked back into the bedroom and took his place next to gently weeping Catherine, his mistress.

Chapter 6

C.J.s Café

As the days passed, Cathy knew she had to get her life back on track. She had ghosts waiting for her near the museum, the Opening of the Portal was getting closer. It was no use moping around in her apartment, over thinking the situation. She knew from Adam, that they were all in separate bedrooms at the house, so she felt sure, there was no romance blossoming between her boyfriend and his ex-wife.

Wandering through the mill corridors, Cathy ventured out to the café. Going in through the door off the corridor, she made her way to the table set up away from the main customers. Becki and Inese saw her and made a beeline to her. "How are you, are you ok?" they both asked.

"I am fine. Any updates on the social media front?" Cathy asked.

"Nothing more than what we found the other day. I am monitoring the cruise ship, it looks like a month-long cruise, nice for some." Inese told Cathy. "No sign of the boy either."

"I did a search to see if any young child had passed away, just to cover that scenario, but didn't find anything." Becki updated Cathy. "Usual order Cathy?"

"Yes please, I didn't think to search to see if the boy had passed on. The Magical Police agency are running a search on missing children and school attendance records, covering the next few valleys to start with. I don't think the sister moved far away. I think that is part of Tamara's lies." Cathy told them.

Cathy sat and sipped at her hazelnut latte; she was interrupted by a gentle cough. Looking up she saw Peter the archaeologist stood in front of her.

"I am sorry to interrupt Cathy, and also sorry to hear what's been going on. But before this started, Adam asked me about the old canal lock in Upper Valley. Well, I have been doing a bit of research myself, and it turns out, when the lock was being constructed an accident occurred." He spoke quietly, as if not wanting people to hear.

"Please sit down, I am sorry to say, I had quite forgotten about the two navvies that were stood next to the lock, when we visited the museum. My minds been all over the place." Cathy explained.

"I quite understand." Peter said sitting next to her and drinking the coffee Becki had quietly slipped in front of him.

"Tell me about the canal, please." Cathy asked him. "Some background information."

"Well, where do I start. The Huddersfield Narrow Canal. It is more or less twenty miles in length, running from Huddersfield to the edge Nether Valley. The canal was planned and passed to be built at the end of the 18th century. But it wasn't completed until around 1811, that was mainly to them having to cut their way through the hill at the Standege Tunnel, just at the furthest edge of upper Valley. (The longest, highest, and deepest tunnel in the UK for a long time."

As it was late in the day for canals, it was never a huge success, and the railways made moving goods by canal outdated before it really began. In 1944, the canal was closed to boats, and was soon overgrown and forgotten. It is fully functional nowadays, after a large clean-up operation around the millennium. A lot of casualties happened in the building of this canal. The navvies first came to the valleys, to build to dig these 'navigations' that the term navvy originated."

"Wow, so much history, and such a shame it wasn't used to its full potential. Sad about the casualties. I bet that long tunnel took some building." Cathy was intrigued, nothing like a new quest to help her mind get back into gear.

"Yes, alongside the canal tunnel though are railway tunnels. When we clear up the lock archaeology, we can move to the tunnels at a later date." Peter agreed.

"What do you mean. The canal lock archaeology?" Cathy asked.

"Well, it just so happens, that the locks going through Upper Valley are due a clean-up, so I put in an application to see if I could so a quick archaeological dig. I looked for deaths along the canal area, in Upper Valley, and found two brothers had disappeared after a night out in Upper Valley, celebrating the opening of the canal, early. Filling in the research, from what Adam told me, I have pieced together, that the following day, the locks were filled with water, and no one noticed the two bodies down in the bottom of the lock. The brothers were called Gabriel and Adebayo Kershaw. The family reported them missing soon after, but no one thought of the canal lock."

Cathy listened to Peter, "You seem to have taken over some of my researching," she giggled. "It is addictive, isn't it?"

"Very much so. So, The small trial dig, starts tomorrow, and I wondered if you want to put your wellies on and join me in a muddy two-hundred-year-old canal lock?" Peter laughed at the invitation.

"Well, how can a girl refuse, I am doing nothing else at the moment. Some archaeology, before the Santa Season would be wonderful. Oh no," Cathy's voice took in a family walking into the café.

"What is it?" Peter asked, "Oh no, that women. I remember from when she married Adam. She was always on the lookout for the next husband, She even tried it on with me! Do you want to leave?"

"No, it's ok, she doesn't know about Adam and me, so I have to behave as if he is just a member of the local community." Cathy then told Peter about how Adam had said that she asked about the rich bitch that owned the place.

"I need to ask Adam about the dig tomorrow, will you be ok, if I go over." Peter asked cautiously.

"Actually, I think, I will come with you. It will do me good to have a secret look at the enemy." Cathy laughed, sounding much braver than she felt.

Finishing off their drinks, Cathy and Peter wandered over to the cute family group sat in one of the sixties style diner's cubicles.

"Sorry to disturb you Adam, but could I have a word with you. I have a new archaeological dig starting tomorrow and I need to run it by the police." Peter asked.

"Hi Peter, Cathy," Adam replied, a little taken aback to see them together, "Sure, what do you need to know?"

"Oh, just the usual parking restrictions and traffic controls. It will only be for a couple of days, whilst the canal lock is being repaired." Peter laughed as Adam cottoned on to the whole reason for the dig.

"That shouldn't be a problem, Tamara, you, and Barney, will be ok for a few hours, whilst I attend the work with Peter. You remember Peter, don't you?" Adam asked his ex-wife.

"Oh hi, I didn't recognise you, is this your wife?" Tamara asked of Cathy.

"Hi Tamara, long time no see. No, this is my good friend Cathy Collins. She is quite new in the area," Peter smirked as he saw Tamara take in Cathy. They all could tell she hadn't heard of Cathy Collins, Lead Witch, ghost whisperer, and owner of most of Green Valley.

"Hi, pleased to meet you, I am Cathy," she held out her hand to shake with Tamara, who was a bit reluctant, but Cathy held her hand out. She wanted to get a feel of this woman, and to use her magic to see what was behind her game.

Reluctantly, Tamara took Cathy's hand and shook it, '*wow, she is a troubled person*,' Cathy thought to herself.

"And you young man, who are you?" Cathy smiled at the little boy, trying to hide in the huge milkshake.

"Hi, I am, err, Barney," the small boy squeaked.

Rather than worry the boy, Cathy shook his hand too, and boy did he feel scared. "Enjoy your milkshake Barney, I must get off."

"Cathy," the small boy asked her. "What is an archaeology dig? Is it like the ones they have on telly?"

Cathy smiled at the boy, who could only be about six or seven. "Do you watch the TV programmes about the archaeology digs."

"Yes," he muttered, "I like dinosaurs, and they dig them up."

"Well, yes, it is that sort of a dig, but there won't be any dinosaurs to be found here. Only the stuff from old canal boats at the most." Peter helped Cathy with this unexpected turn of events.

"But I do have a dinosaur tooth that I dug up once, if I can find it, I will give it to Adam for you. Will that be ok with you Tamara. Fancy you with a son, that likes dinosaurs," Peter smirked, as he remembered Tamara didn't like getting her hands dirty.

Adam nodded and laughed too, "That would be great Barney, I have some books too, we could perhaps have a look at them together."

"Oh wow, thank you," Barney said with a little more confidence, as Cathy could tense Tamara gently boiling inside.

"We must be off, see you at the dig, 10.00am prompt, at the museum car park." Peter held Cathy's arm, and the pair left the café by the main entrance.

"Well, my money is on that boy belonging to her sister. Her husband is an old colleague, and was obsessed with dinosaurs, and that must be where he got his interest." Peter told her.

"That was a good ploy, going over. I will admit, I was petrified, but feel so much better now, I met them myself. Well tomorrow will be fun. I best get back to the Temple Room and prepare for Gabriel and Adebayo to be reunited with their families. Thank you, Peter, you have helped more than you will ever know." Cathy hugged him and saw Adam coming out of the Café with Tamara scowling at Barney.

"I will pick you up at 9.00am, make sure you wear your scruffy old clothes for going into the old lock." Peter kissed her gently on her cheek, as Cathy wandered back inside the mill, to update her Gran on the day's proceedings. *"Well, that was an experience,"* she thought to herself. *'That woman is lying, but the question is WHY?'*

Arriving back at the apartment, she found her Gran and Oskar, and brought them up to date on her visit to the café.

"Cathy, are you alright, how was the woman?" Oskar asked her, with concern.

"She was as I imagined, my sixth sense says she is lying through her teeth, but why?" Cathy confided.

"Time will tell, but at least you and Adam are ok, when all this is over." Sally said.

"He actually looked quite put out, that I was with Peter. Oh, I am off on an archaeology dig tomorrow," Cathy excitedly told them. "Nothing like helping a couple of ghosts to take my mind of things. I am going to try and do some research now; I have an early start tomorrow. care to help?!"

"Absolutely, what are we researching now?" Sally asked.

"The Canal being built and the two ghosts we saw at the Mabon party, at the Upper Valley Museum." Cathy told her. "They are brothers, called Gabriel and Adebayo Kershaw. To be honest, Peter has done most of the research for me, but I just thought I would have a look, and forget Adam for a while."

"I understand. Yes, the canal, it is busier now, than when it was originally built," Oskar input into the conversation.

"Just how old are you?" laughed Cathy.

"Old enough," replied Oskar with his usual smirk.

"Oskar, stop teasing Cathy," laughed Sally. "I think Peter has filled you in on most of the history of the canal. I believe you can now holiday on a canal barge, and the marina at the far end of Green Valley is a busy place.

"Yes, it has a new development of hoses, and a new boat house, which is apartments, I believe. Next door to the pub and the supermarket, good place for a canal holiday boat to stop." Cathy agreed. "Peter and Susie are picking me up in the morning, so I can join the dig. Isn't that exciting, we are quite the archaeology ghost finding team."

"It is all part of your role Cathy, as the ghost whisperer. I am extremely proud of how you are handling it. Some people would have run away, being confronted constantly with ghosts."

"I guess it is in my DNA, gran." Cathy laughed, "Now, you two, tell me everything you know about the canal from Huddersfield to Ashton Under Lyne, that runs through our Green Valleys."

Chapter 7

The Canal

Cathy used magic to get dressed, if she was going climbing down into old canal locks, she certainly wasn't dressing like a fashion statement. Comfy jeans, thick socks, and strong wellington boots.

She was ready, after a good breakfast, for when Peter and Susie, picked her up from her mill apartment. *'How does this old Land Rover keeps going?'* Cathy thought to herself, as she climbed into the back, amongst all the toolboxes and equipment.

"Hi Cathy," Susie greeted her, "Welcome on another adventure."

"An adventure, indeed," Cathy laughed, "First it was the workhouse and the mill ghosts. Next airplane crashes and the packhorse bridge. Now we are heading into a drained canal lock. I never realised how in demand a ghost whisperer would be."

"Yes, I agree, it has been busy for you," Susie agreed. "But think of all those poor souls, you have helped become at peace. You really are a star."

"Thanks Susie," Cathy agreed. "What is the plan for today? You seem to be the assistant ghost whisperer now."

"Oh, I like that title," Susie laughed. "It sounds much better than the 'Finds Table Lady.' David and Nigel have been at the site for a couple of days, preparing the area. The water board have drained the lock to start some repair work. We have just today to do the archaeological report. It is only twenty years or so, since the lock was last drained, when the canal was reopened for canal boats again."

"What I would like to do, is have a look around the immediate area, for the any sign of the ghosts of the two brothers. I don't imagine any of their remains are here, as they would have been found on previous digs. But it is an ideal time to try and contact them and try to talk and find out any more history that we can." Cathy told Susie.

"Look, they have erected a huge canvas over the dry lock. To keep away prying eyes away." Susie pointed to the site. "Although, I bet it has the opposite effect, as people will wander over to see what is happening."

As the old land rover approached the museum car park, Cathy noticed the car park was empty again. "Is this car park always empty?" She asked her companions.

"Only when you are in town," Peter laughed. He parked the land rover in a space nearest the lock. The group then put on their workwear and Hi-Vis jackets, then made their way over to the dig, to be met by David.

"Morning folks," he greeted them. "Nigel is knee deep in mud at the bottom of the lock. But it is drying out slowly."

"Good morning, David," Cathy smiled, this was her friend Gillian's partner now. Werewolf by nature, although Cathy had never seen his brother or him shifting. "Have you found anything yet?"

"Nothing at all in the lock, it was cleaned out in the renovations. We are digging a trial trench, just to be sure," he laughed. "No sign of any ghosts though."

"I am sure they will appear now that Cathy is here." Peter replied. "Come on let's go and have a look at the dig. We haven't got long to work on this site."

As they neared the covered area of the lock, Peter went to talk to the waterboard representatives.

"Come on Cathy, shall we go and explore." Susie pulled Cathy excitedly towards the opening of the tent.

"Are you coming with us, and not just waiting for finds?" Cathy teased Susie, while she tried to keep up with her, racing towards the tent.

"I don't think we will find very much. To be honest, this is just a cover to help you find the two ghosts. Peter was so intrigued with the canal history when he started his research. You open a door for him to the actual events that happened. A portal to the past he calls it." Susie confided in Cathy.

They opened the gap in the side of the canvas. In front of them was the old canal lock which looked a lot bigger and deeper now that there was no water in it.

They gingerly climb down the ladders into what Cathy expected to be a muddy bath.

"Oh, it doesn't feel half as muddy as I expected." Cathy laughed as she stepped into the empty space.

"We have moved a lot of the muds sifting through each bucket. But nothing unexpected, the usual beer cans and crisp packets and even a shoe, well the modern trainer," Nigel told them.

"What do you want me to do?" Cathy asked her colleagues.

"Use your magic," Suzy teased.

"Well, I guess I could call on my sixth sense, see what or has been in the old canal lock." Cathy agreed. Peter, David, Nigel, and Suzy formed a semi-circle around Cathy. She breathed in deep a few times and called out to see if anyone or the girls were around.

"I can't feel anything," she told her friends.

"Keep trying, Cathy," Peter assured her, "we are all here for you."

"Gabriel and Adebayo Kershaw, please show yourself to me. You appeared the other week, please show yourself again. I am Cathy Collins, the ghost whisper." Cathy asked the empty air of the lock.

Cathy surveyed the surroundings, twenty foot down a drained canal lock, the huge double wood doors at the far end kept out a vast amount of water away from them. *"Scary,"* she thought to herself.

"Gabriel and Adebayo, are you here, please make yourselves visible. My colleagues and I are here to help you pass over." Cathy tried again.

Whilst she stood trying to feel the breeze of the two ghosts, her mind flashed a thought to a certain place on the canal lock wall. "What is that over there?" She pointed to the archaeologists.

"Show us Cathy, we can't see things like you can?" David asked her.

"Here, just in this space, I can sense something is hidden here. Don't ask me how I know, blame it on the sixth sense," she laughed. "Do you have one of those small radar things, that you use?"

"Yes, we have a portable ground radar machine, shall I go and retrieve it from the Land Rover?" Peter asked.

"Please, I have an image of a box, or something hidden in the wall. I am sorry I can't be clearer, but it's just the image I have in my mind." Cathy apologised.

"You keep trying, I will be back as soon as I can," and Peter climbed the ladder out of the drained lock.

David and Nigel, strode over to the area that Cathy had pointed out.

"Is this the area?" they asked. "Do you want us to have a look?"

"Yes, I am sorry, but all I keep seeing is a small metallic box." Cathy told them. "I will go nearer and try to see if I can feel anything else." *"I wonder what it signifies?"* she thought to herself.

"Are there any ghosts here, that can help me find out what the box is used for, and why I am being led towards this area?" She chanted to herself, trying to get the ghostly brothers to show themselves.

"Gradually she felt the cool breeze circulating around her. She smiled because she knew the sign of ghosts being nearby.

Holding onto Susie's hand, she gave it a gentle squeeze; to let her know she had made some form of contact.

"Please can you make yourselves visible. We are here to help you," Cathy told the very faint visions of two men at the farthest part of the lock. "We are friendly, Gabriel and Adebayo, these are your names?"

Peter arrived back with the portable radar, having already taken it out of the carrying case, so it was ready to use. "Where do you want me to start the search?" he asked Cathy.

"Here," Cathy pointed to a place near the top of the lock, "You will need to go on the ladder to do the radar."

"Gabriel, can you tell me why the box is so important, is it yours?" Cathy asked the outline of the ghosts.

"Can you....?" Peter stuttered, "Can you see them?" Susie nodded to him, and let Cathy continue with the talking.

"Gabriel, what is in the box, Peter can help us find it for you?"
Cathy left the group and walked down the length of the dry dock,
towards the double door of the lock gate.

"Please show yourself," Cathy asked, mainly to herself. She
felt herself in the middle of a lot of mixed-up cool swirling
breezes. She thought that at least the two brothers were with her.

A shout from the other end of the dry lock, made Cathy do a
quick turn,

"We have seen something on the radar, Cathy," Peter shouted.

"Come with me Gabriel and Adebayo, you can tell us what is
so special that is in the box. Or we can just leave it where it is."
Cathy said trying to get the two ghostly outlines to follow her.

Whilst she walked the small distance to her colleagues, she
felt the two ghosts slowly becoming visible to everyone.

"They are our medals in the tin," the tallest brother told Cathy.

"Hello," Cathy turned to them both and stretched out her hand
to shake hands with them.

"How can you touch us?" The tall one asked.

"I am Cathy Collins, the ghost whisperer." Cathy smiled.
"And you are?"

"I am Gabe, and this is my younger brother Ade. Please could
you help us find our medals?" Gabe asked.

"Medals, what medals would you have. When did you lose
your lives?" Cathy questioned the pair.

Cathy noticed that the archaeologists were now using the
radar machine, and that they had started to dig in the area she had
pointed out.

"We died in 1811. We were out drinking in The Globe at Old
Neds. We were celebrating the end of the wretched Standedge
Tunnel. The one that is known as the highest, longest, and
deepest tunnel in England. For us it was no more than a death
trap." Ade told her. "We always carried our belongings with us,
we never knew what work we would have one day to the next.
We were canal navvies – the ones that did the hard graft. We were
paid day by day for the work we had done. When the canal was
finally fully opened, we knew we would have to go and find some
more work."

Gabe took over the story, whilst the others listened. "We had
been in the pub and wandered back this way to our lodgings. The

box fell out of the bundle we carried our clothes in. Straight into the lock it went. Ade jumped straight in, and I followed. Neither of us thought about the icy cold water, we were just desperate to get the box back. The cold wintery water snuffed our lives out immediately. We had spent our work tokens at Old Ned's and were worse for wear. We never did find the box and lost our lives trying."

"We have hit something in the wall, feels like metal," shouted Peter. "I am going to try to move it."

"Please be careful," Gabe cried, "Our lives are in that box."

"It is ok, he can see you, as can the others. With you being with me, we can all see you. I am the ghost whisperer," she whispered. "Shall we go and join them and see the box?" Cathy led them towards the others.

Cathy introduced the two brothers to the archaeologists, while Peter gently removed the box from its two hundred year hiding place.

"That is our box," exclaimed Gabe.

"Please see if you can open it," Ade asked, "I don't think we can touch anything."

Peter passed the box to Cathy, it was about eight inches square, and three inches deep.

"It looks a little bit squashed," She told the ghosts.

"Please open it, we have been looking for our belongings and medals for years." Gabe said.

Prising the rusty lid off the box, Cathy saw inside a lot of mud, with what appeared to be medals inside.

"Wow, these look impressive," she told them. "There are medals and some coins inside the box."

Handing the contents to Susie, they cleaned the soil and mud off them, to reveal a set of medals.

"What are the medals from?" Cathy asked the excited brothers.

"We have two each, the 1802 is the Manchester and the Salford Volunteer medal." Gabe explained to them. "the other one is the 1805 medal, that we got for fighting at Trafalgar."

"We fought for our King and the Country. I was injured, so we left the volunteers. That was when we got the sovereigns for our pay." Ade took up the story. "We then had to find work to be able to survive. So ever since we have been navvies building the canals. We kept the sovereigns and medals safe in our belongings. The tin held our life in it. For emergencies. When it slipped out of the bag that night, well our world ended there and then."

"You were at the battle of Trafalgar?" Peter asked in awe.

"Yes, we were aboard one of the ships, it wasn't very pleasant." Gabe sighed. "We went overseas and were actually incredibly lucky to return back to England. The work we had sought afterwards brought us to Upper Valley. We adore the area and even though we were billeted in a small wooden hut, we were thinking of staying in the area. Give up the wandering around."

Whilst Peter spent the next few minutes quizzing the two ghosts. An archaeologists dream came true for him. Cathy and Susie cleaned the contents of the tin.

"What would you like us to do with the contents and the box?" Cathy asked Gabe and Ade.

"The museum is a fascinating place," Gabe told her. "We have been in a lot since it was built. Do you think it would be possible for our story and box to have a small display. We don't have any descendants, neither of us were married. So, to see our story live on forever, well that would be our reward."

"That would be an excellent idea, Susie can you do a sketch of the brothers, so we can have an 'Artist Impression' of them, to go with the display." Cathy asked her.

"Would you do that for us?" Gabe questioned.

"Of course, if you want us to." Cathy replied. "Do you want to pass over and be at peace now?"

"Oh yes please. We have stayed here so long, waiting for our medals to be found." Ade spoke for the pair.

"We don't have long left; because the water people want to start to refill the lock soon." Peter interrupted.

"Right, shall we get as much information as we can before we have to perform the passing over ceremony. "Cathy asked,

David and Nigel did some more digging and found some more belonging of the brothers. Cathy, Susie, and Peter chatted to the two-hundred-year-old travellers.

Questions like - How life was back in 1800s. The payment they received daily for being a navvy, was a paper note/ token that could be spent locally at the pubs or food cabins.

Eventually the call came from the waterboard, up above that their time was nearly up. With it approaching dusk outside, it was agreed to wait until the waterboard employees had done their work and left the scene. Before the passing over ceremony would begin.

Moving over towards the museum car park, Cathy and the two ghostly brothers waited patiently for the work to be completed.

When the area was quiet again, Cathy saw the two brothers hug each other close. She realised that they were saying goodbye to each other.

"You will be together when you pass over," she gently told them.

"Are you sure?" Gabe asked, quite tearful.

"Yes, I can assure you, you will go together, to whatever is waiting on the other side. I have seen it happen a few times now." Cathy reassured them both.

Holding tight to the box, containing the medals and coins, Cathy got her bag of witchy things from the Land Rover.

The small group had gathered at the side of the lock, on the canal towpath, away from prying eyes.

Cathy laid out her equipment, while Peter, Susie, David, and Nigel formed a semi-circle. She set out the pentagon and candles, in the same positions as she had been taught before. She placed the medals and coins in the centre of the pentagon.

Taking a deep breath, she held the hands of the two ghosts. She said the 'Freedom to Pass' spell, and she watched the faces of Gabe and Ade. She told them to relax and go and join their loved ones on the other side.

Slowly the young navvies faded into the air, as they passed over, finally.

"Cathy, you never cease to amaze. What a story we have uncovered. To actually converse with the ghosts of over two hundred years ago. Well, it is incredible. To think they served at the Battle of Trafalgar." Peter glowed.

"We will have to put on a special display for them, at the museum. I know the curator very well, so that won't be a problem." Susie told them.

"I will come with you to see them. At the Mabon festival, we had a tour of the museum, and I felt a few cold spots that I would like to go back to." Cathy laughed.

"Only on one condition," Peter teased.

"What is that?" Cathy asked curiously.

"That I can come with you, you aren't going finding ghosts without me." He smiled.

"And me," joined in the other three.

"Now, shall we get Cathy home so she can recharge her batteries, she has used a lot of energy recently." Susie steered the group back to the vehicles. "I have reports and pictures to draw too."

"Who will look after the medals?" Cathy asked them.

"Err, well, I guess we had better take them to Adam and the Magical Police. They will care for them until we can get the secure display sorted at the museum." Peter replied.

"Ok, I understand," sighed Cathy. "Can you take them, I don't want to go near that house, while that woman is living there."

"So sorry Cathy," Susie held her hand tight. "I am sure it will all get sorted out soon. Like Peter said, he is sure that young boy is the son of an old colleague called Bob."

"I do hope so," Cathy felt weary now. "it just seems to be taking forever to get her to slip up. I know Adam is doing what he can, for the boy if nothing else."

"Here we are back at the mill, we are at your apartment Cathy." Peter stopped the Land Rover next to the shop doorway. "Will you be alright?"

"I will be fine. I want to write up what I can remember, shower, and then bath. But food first, we haven't eaten properly all day." Cathy laughed as she climbed out of the passenger side.

Sally and Clara Jane were waiting for her, as she let herself into the apartment. Cathy had to tell them all about the day and the results.

"So, Clara Jane, two ghosts much older than you." Cathy laughed. "Sorry, but I am really shattered, and I think I will actually sleep well tonight. Peter and Susie have taken the medals around to Adam's house. I couldn't face it with her still being there."

"We will be around and look after you," Sally told her. "Get your food eaten, shower and then drink this special brew before you get into bed. I know you are tired, but the drink will just help you along."

Chapter 8

Auntie Tamara's Ring

Cathy was still on a high from meeting the canal brothers and the vampire brothers. The work that Fillipe was working on was very impressive. Cathy was in her Temple Room, with her grimoire. Trying to work out the final magical missing piece of the vampire jigsaw.

Her latest adventures had boosted her moral. She couldn't hurry things along with Adam and Tamara. It was out of her hands what she could do. Everyone was of the opinion that the child was her sister's boy. But no one could prove it. The search for the elusive second husband, Bill McIlroy had proved fruitless, but the MPA had asked their counterparts in the USA to do a search. The sister and husband were still on their cruise, and the MPA couldn't contact them, whilst out of the country. Social media had hit a brick wall.

So, Cathy had no choice but to manage one day to the next. She saw Adam occasionally, but not to talk to, it was though he was under a spell from Tamara.

The vampires had made her so welcome, she thought about the two young boys, Mikael, and Izaak. Their impeccable manners and their longing to play football outside in the sunshine.,

Cathy let the grimoire rest on her knee, while she drifted into a practised meditation. Throughout the meditation, she felt that she could hear Gillian whispering to her. She woke with a start, as the messages seem to be getting more anxious.

She soon realised that Gillian was actually telling her to come to the shop. Tamara and young Barney were looking around the displays of crystals.

"*Keep hidden,*" Gillian telepathed to Cathy. "*They don't know you own the business.*"

"Alright, I will stay in the shadows, are you ok?" she telepathed back.

"Yes, I am fine, but she is asking a lot of questions, I want you to come and listen. I have the CCTV recording it too." Gillian replied. *"It is fantastic the ability of sending messages to each other."*

Cathy left the Temple Room and walked down the corridor the towards the workroom and then through to the back of the shop. Clara Jane was busy creating her jewellery. Cathy raised her finger to her lips, indicating that she remained quiet. "Follow me," she whispered.

The pair went into the shadows of the selling area of the business. They hid behind a partition that had been set there previously.

"So, you are the owner of this shop?" They heard Tamara question Gillian.

"Yes, this is my small shop, I usually sell my crystals at local fairs or festivals." Gillian replied.

"Do you know the woman that owns half of Green Valley?" Tamara asked.

"I am not sure I know who you are talking about," Gillian innocently replied.

"The one that is making a fool of herself chasing my husband." Tamara spat out.

Spying Barney looking into a display cabinet, Gillian discreetly tried to change the subject.

"Hi young man. Have you seen anything you like?" she asked him.

"Excuse me, but I asked you a question!" Tamara snapped.

"If you mean Cathy, yes, I do know her. Why do you ask?" Gillian told her.

Cathy and Clara Jane waited for the answer and smiled at each other.

"I want to know what that rich bitch wants with my husband." Tamara snarled.

"Sorry," Gillian said quietly. "But I was under the impression that the two of you had divorced and that you had in fact remarried."

Avoiding the remark, Tamara carried on, "Well I am back now, and back to stay. I am back with OUR son. You tell her to stay away from him. He is my property now."

Gillian was a little taken aback at the aggressiveness of the woman. *"What game is she playing?"* she telepathed to Cathy.

"No idea, try the boy again. Show him the animal crystals that we have, the crystals for young kids." Cathy told her. *"*A*sk her what stone her ring is. It is doing a lot of sparkling, but it isn't a diamond."*

"What an amazing ring?" Gillian said to Tamara, "What stone is set in the ring?"

"You are asking me about a stone when you are supposed to be the expert." Tamara wasn't a pleasant woman.

"I was just admiring it, as it sparkled so much in the shop." Gillian tried to get her to open up.

"It is a diamond you stupid woman." Tamara sniggered as she got the upper hand, or thought she had.

"Don't say anything," Cathy mentally told Gillian. *"We know it isn't, but don't upset her. Try the boy again."*

Gillian sauntered over to where barney was looking at a display cabinet. Tamara was looking at herself in one of the display mirrors. *"How vain!"* Cathy thought.

"Cute aren't they, the animals. The elephant is made from a crystal call Lapis Lazuli. The green owl is made from a crystal called Malachite. Would you like one to take with you?" Gillian asked him.

"I am not sure if I am allowed." The boy uttered his first words. Cathy and Gillian were both surprised at the young boy, he appeared petrified of Tamara.

"Auntie Tam, I mean Mummy," he spluttered, "Can I have one of these owls please." He cowered next to Gillian. He looked up at her, his littles eyes pleading at her. Gillian put her hand on his shoulder to reassure him and whispered, "She didn't hear you."

Barney looked up at Gillian as if to say thank you. "It will be ok; we will get you sorted soon." Gillian slipped him the small owl. "Keep this safe and he will help you too."

"Right, Barney, we must get back to Daddy, he will be wondering where we are. He misses us so much when we are not with him." She turned round to leave the shop, and she caught sight of Barney stood with Gillian.

Gillian bent down to tell Barney if he needed anything to ask Adam. He was a good man and will look after him.

"Come along boy, what is it with you?" Tamara grabbed his arm and practically dragged him out of the shop.

When they had left the shop, Cathy and Clara Jane came out from their hiding place and into the shop front.

"Well, I assume all that was on CCTV," Cathy laughed, she felt a weight was lifting off her shoulders, after Barney's little slip up.

"I most certainly have, and I recorded it on my phone too, just in case." Gillian smiled.

"What was that ring, I am sure it is the stone I need for the vampires experiment?" Cathy asked.

"I think it is a very pale citrine. I nearly asked if it was clear quartz, but her reaction from me asking was enough. But it is a small yellow like citrine, I am sure. A sunshine glow!" Gillian smiled at Cathy.

"Have we caught two birds with one stone?" Cathy laughed. "I certainly feel better from witnessing that performance. That poor child is petrified. I will message Adam to update him on this meeting."

"We just need her husband and the sister too." Clara Jane laughed. "Then we can fit all the pieces of the jigsaw together."

"I will also get a copy of the CCTV and pass it onto Brian and the MPA, poor child, he would have been in trouble if she had heard him call her Auntie Tam," laughed Gillian.

"Auntie Tam it is. Phew let us hope it all gets sorted out soon, I miss him," sighed Cathy. "But shall we order some extra citrine to test out for the vampires. Also, let's get some moonstones in stock too. Sunny glow and moonstone. I like that idea."

Chapter 9

Samhain / Halloween

Cathy and Gillian were closing the shop early. They were going to the Nether Valley Coven, Samhain party.

"How have we got to the end of October already?" asked Gillian.

"I have no idea; time seems to be flying by these days. At least it has been quiet and no more threats from Tamara." Cathy sighed. "Adam text me to say that Barney has spoken a bit more to him. Mainly about dinosaurs and what the police do. But there is no news from the MPA."

"I am sure it will be all over soon," Gillian reassured her. "Right, I am going to take Marley home and will be back in the cab about 7 o'clock. I am looking forward to another night with our neighbouring covens. What a better night to meet than Halloween and Samhain."

After Gillian had left, Cathy locked the shop and made her way back along the corridor to her own apartment. She was getting used to living back at the mill. She just couldn't see how or when Tamara would be caught out. Even though she got the occasional message off Adam, she felt he was slipping away from her.

To keep herself occupied until it was time to go out, she thought she would try experimenting with the new stock of citrine and moonstones. *"Time for half an hour in the Temple Room,"* she thought to herself.

Entering the temple Room, Cathy relaxed immediately. Clara Jane and Sally came into vision and asked how she was.

"What time does the fun start?" Clara Jane asked her. "What shall I wear?"

The young ghost was now able to go to all the events, her ties from the mill all but disappeared, but she must still be accompanied by Sally.

"Not until 7.00pm," Cathy relied. "I was going to wear black trousers and a lacy top. It is the end of October, so not that warm outdoors."

"That is what I was thinking. Cathy see you later." Clara Jane laughed and disappeared.

"How are you, Cathy?" Oskar asked her.

"I am alright, I guess." Cathy sighed, "I just wish everything was back to normal. But I just cannot think how we can trap Tamara. But, on a brighter note, I do think I am on a breakthrough for the vampires. I am thinking that a mix of citrine and moonstone, but do I slice or grind the crystal into a powder? It has to mix with the silicon for the chip."

For the next hour or so, Cathy, Sally and Oskar looked at the crystals and chatted about various options.

Eventually Cathy admitted, it was time to go and prepare herself for the Samhain event. She couldn't muster any enthusiasm, but she knew that because she was the head of the coven, she didn't have much of a personal life.

At 7.00pm., Sally and Clara Jane appeared; to let her know they would meet her at the Nether Valley headquarters. Minutes later, she heard the taxi outside, with Gillian waiting for her.

"Enjoy yourself and try to relax, Cathy." Oskar told her.

"Thanks, Oskar. I will be home soon." Cathy smiles and left to join Gillian. Soon the taxi was driving up a very steep driveway, towards the home of the Nether Valley Coven.

When they arrived outside the aptly named "Nether Valley Hall," Cathy let out a gasp. "Wow, this is an impressive old building. It is more like a stately home."

"Look, Bronwen is waiting for us, at the top of an impressing set of stone steps." Gillian pointed to a figure at the entrance to the hall.

They paid the taxi driver and headed towards their host for the evening.

"Welcome to nether Valley Hall." Bronwen greeted them.

"It looks an amazing place." Cathy told her.

"The hall was built between 1861 and 1864, by the local cotton mill owner, Mr Mayall. It was their home unit around 1891. The council then bought it and made it their Town hall. It was purchased by the coven, back in 1986. Most of us have apartments here, similar to the apartments at Riverside Mill." Bronwen explained. "Come along inside. The hallway is just as impressive."

Bronwen led them through a set of double arched doors, into a mahogany hallway, with a fully painted ceiling.

"You are not wrong," Cathy said. "Just look at that staircase. I love how it splits into two and leads to the upper floors. I can picture ladies, in their long dresses, making an entrance down those stairs."

Looking around Cathy could see various doorways leading off the hall, in a symmetrical pattern on each side of the hall.

Bronwen led them to the first door on the left-hand side. The two women were speechless when they walked into the room. A fantastic huge, ballroom was decorated in blacks and orange. Halloween colours, and Samhain decorations. The idea of this party was to combine the Halloween and Samhain festivals.

"Ladies, and guests. Our friends have arrived, so shall we get the party started?" Bronwen told the crowd of witches, and friends.

"First, we will celebrate the traditions of Halloween, as it is the 31st of October. After midnight we will change our celebrations to Samhain. We shall drink to the end of summer and signal the beginning of winter. It is acknowledged that Samhain is a time when the 'doorway to the otherworld opens.' Allowing supernatural beings and the souls of the dead to come into our world. Samhain is also called the Festival of the Dead." Bronwen continued. "We should be fine this evening if that happens. Because we have Cathy the Ghost Whisperer in our midst."

"Thanks," laughed Cathy. "I was hoping for a night off."

"Oh, you don't get a night off, not with your powers," laughed Gillian.

"Come along, shall we go and get some drinks. I am afraid I cannot offer you the juniper tea, like Upper Valley." Bronwen laughed and led them to a large table, at the end of the room. It was overloaded with drinks and food.

"Thank goodness, it took me days to get over the juniper tea," Gillian groaned.

"We do have our special recipe mulled cider punch though!"
Bronwen offered than two glasses of warm cider. "Do not drink
it too fast, it is quite potent. We also have Wassail, this is cider
with sliced fruit and brandy."

After about an hour, Bronwen called everyone to attention.
"Ladies and Gentlemen, now that everyone has arrived, I would
like to welcome everyone here to the Festival of Samhain. During
the evening we will be having a few games, that everyone will
join in. An ice breaker and to get everyone in the party mood. At
midnight we will be lighting the bonfire, outside of course.
Before we start, I would like to make a small offering of various
food and goods, to protect us from bad spirits.

'Tonight, we honour our ancestors and their souls.
We give thanks for our harvest.
We know you watch us always.
Protecting and guarding us.
Tonight, we think of you, as always.'

When the prayers and offerings were completed, Cathy asked
Bronwen if it was possible to have a tour of the hall and the other
rooms.

"Absolutely, I will get one of the girls to give you a guided
tour, She know the place well, as she lives here too." Bronwen
went to fetch her friend, Kirsty.

Soon, Cathy, Gillian and a couple of others were being given
a guided tour of the Nether Valley Town Hall.

Leaving the ballroom, Kirsty led then in and out of various
doors and rooms. They saw offices, lounges, even the kitchen
was decorated in the ornate style of the hall.

"We are not officially allowed in this room, but I am sure we
will be all right this evening. "Kirsty said, unlocking a double set
of doors, that mirrored the ballroom opposite.

"That looks a big key?" Gillian giggled. "It is massive, what
is behind these doors that needs such a key?"

"Let me show you," Kirsty laughed.

"I think these two have had too much punch already," thought
Cathy, with a warning feeling descending on her.

Opening the door, and switching on the bright lights, Cathy
was also dumbstruck. "What is this place?" she asked, whilst
looking round at a court room. Matching mahogany furniture and

the decoration. But in front of her was a raised platform, that was obviously where a judge would sit.

"It is the old courtroom. When the council bought the hall, they had this room enlarges and built the court room. There is the judges chair and the witness box over there." Kirsty was in her element showing off this hidden gem. "In the early 20th century, it was used as the courtroom for the area,"

"Why isn't it used, or open to the public?" Cathy asked, although her gut feeling told her that she knew the answer already – ghosts.

"The courtroom was used for inquests in the early 1900s. For a time, the police station was held in the ballroom area. Yes, it was made into smaller offices and prison cells." Kirsty was enjoying being the tour guide.

"What happened?" Cathy carried on asking questions.

"A prisoner escaped from the police cell, and caused rampage through the police station, and made it into the court room. He was eventually restrained, but not until after he had managed to grab a knife and stabbed the judge, that was sitting on the day. It was decided after that to move the police station, to its current place. The judge died of his wounds, and it is said he haunts the room." Kirsty beamed at Cathy, as she mentioned ghosts.

"I see, and that is why we are in here, to see if I can feel or sense anything." Cathy commented, with disappointment in her voice.

"What on earth is going on in here?" a voice shouted from the doorway. Bronwen stood at the door, looking terribly angry. "Kirsty, you know that no one is allowed in this room."

"But I thought that…" Kirsty tried to say.

"You just thought that because Cathy is our guest tonight, that you would bring her in here to find the ghost. Didn't you?" Bronwen was not happy.

"Yes, but why not?" Kirsty mumbled.

"Because she is our guest for the Samhain Festival. She is not here to work. I was going to ask her to come and visit, another time. Why can you not just let things occur naturally. I am deeply sorry ladies, but the tour is at an end for now. Please can we all make our way back to the ballroom."

Catching up with Cathy, Bronwen put her hand on her arm. "I am so sorry, so sorry that we have imposed on you." Bronwen was mortified that one of her own had stepped out of line.

"Bronwen, please do not get upset. No harm has been done. It is a fantastic room, and I would love to come back soon. But in all honesty, I couldn't feel anything in there." Cathy held her hand out to shake to confirm she wasn't offended.

While they walked across the entrance hall, Bronwen held Cathy back to whisper to her. "What they don't know is, that the judge was my great grandfather. I was hoping you could connect us, while I was with you. I am so sorry for this." Bronwen was nearly in tears.

"I can come back anytime when it is just you and myself. I am looking for things to take my mind off Adam and his ex-wife." Cathy confided. "But I may have to bring Peter the archaeologist, as he now is my number one assistant. Any excuse to talk to a ghost. That man is totally history mad."

"Oh brilliant, thank you so much." Bronwen visibly relaxed. "I think we need some more cider. Then it will be your turn at apple bobbing."

They walked back into the ballroom to hear peals of laughter. "Oh my, this sounds fun, what are they doing?" Cathy laughed.

"A mixture of apple bobbing, first you have to get the apple off the top of a pile of flour, and then you have to try to get the pieces of apple, out of the water. It is ultra messy and lots of fun to watch. Not that I partake in it." Bronwen explained.

"Shall we get the cider, or do you want something different?" We need to keep warm, as we will be lighting the bonfire soon. The fireworks will be starting too. looks like everyone else has started the food already," Bronwen pointed to the empty plates.

Cathy wondered how long she had been on the guided tour for. It seemed like a few minutes but now it was heading towards midnight.

She was feeling relaxed, no lost souls had tried to make contact, yet!

Gillian and Kirsty made their way over to Cathy and Bronwen

"I am so sorry," Kirsty said to them both. "I was so excited about Cathy being here this evening."

"Don't worry, everything will be fine." Bronwen told her. "Cathy says she will come over one day next week to have a look around, when it is quieter.

"Phew," Kirsty breathed a sigh of relief.

"Cathy," Gillian said, pulling Cathy towards the centre of the ballroom. "It is your turn for the apple bobbing."

"Nooooo." Cathy squealed. "Not me please."

"I will if you will," Gillian giggled. "Look, Kim and Wendy are just about to take their turn."

"Help," Cathy pleaded. But no one listened, they just led her to the table that had been set up with a pile of flour next to a bowl of water. Towels at the ready.

After getting soaked and covered in flour, Cathy looked around and saw most of the people were in the same dishevelled state, so she went and got some more wine, deciding to just go with the flow.

"Ladies, please help yourselves to the food. The disco will be starting soon and at 11.45pm, we will be heading outside to the rear yard." Bronwen announced.

Cathy sighed with relief; it seemed the courtroom episode had been forgotten. Sally and Clara Jane found Cathy at the food table. "Is everything alright Cathy?" Sally asked.

She updated them on the events of the evening, and it was agreed to forget about it all, until she came back later in the week.

"If that is possible, being All Hallows Eve," Clara Jane added.

"Thank you for the reminder, my favourite teen ghost." Cathy teased.

The party moved outdoors. Cathy, Bronwen and Glynis stood together as the bonfire took hold, and the flames flickered high into the dark night sky.

Fireworks exploded overhead lighting up the whole of the valley, that spread out way below in the valley.

"I am so happy, to have met you both," Cathy told them.

"We are happy we met you too," laughed Glynis. "Just look at Clara Jane."

"Bless her, this is probably her first bonfire and proper fireworks. I cannot imagine how she was stuck in the mill all those years. I bet the noise from the fireworks scared her. She looks so happy now. Getting a sort of life that she can now enjoy." Cathy agreed.

The three ladies linked arms as they watched their coven members enjoying the evening.

"Don't they all look happy?" commented Glynis.

"That is probably down to the mulled cider and the Wassail." Bronwen laughed. "There was rather too much brandy in the last batch!"

The evening was a huge success. Cathy thought about how each coven had their own unique home. The Enchanted Mill, The Museum and now the Nether Valley Town Hall., complete with courtroom.

"That feels like more work for the ghost whisperer," she thought to herself. But she smiled as she realised how she had enjoyed herself, and was thinking less about Adam.

Chapter 10

The Grand Opening of the Portal

Cathy woke the following morning, her head felt quite heavy, but she put it down to the empty apartment she had come home to, and not the mulled wine. She knew she had to get sorter early, this was the day the Portal was officially opened, and she knew Adam would be present.

She strolled into the kitchen and clicked her fingers. Immediately her breakfast was on the breakfast bar waiting for her.

She still smiled when she thought the clicking of her fingers created the magic. She had since found out that it was her own intentions that set the magic. But she clicked the fingers for her own effect.

Oskar arrived, just as Sally and Clara Jane appeared.

"Oh Oskar," laughed Clara Jane. "You should have seen Cathy doing the apple bobbing; it was so funny."

"Funny, I was absolutely soaking and covered in flour. Although, I must admit, everyone was the same. Sun a simple game, but so much fun. Everyone was laughing so much." Cathy agreed.

"How was it left, with the matter of the courtroom?" Sally asked.

"That was embarrassing," Cathy sighed. "Kirsty was so excited that the ghost whisperer was in her company. She just wanted to see what I thought or could feel. But Bronwen was so upset. I could feel the tension between them both. I said I would call back later this week to see if I could sense anything, I did say that I would be taking Peter and Susie. Another chance for him to chat to a ghost."

"That is a great idea. I think Peter and Susie make good sidekicks for the Ghost Whisperer." Sally laughed.

"I can remember my Pa, talking about the judge that was stabbed." Clara Jane spoke up.

"Clara Jane, you are a walking history book." Cathy told her. "Still, I guess I better get ready to go the Opening of the Portal ceremony."

"It is an important date for Riverside Mill. The 1st of November is the official opening of the Santa Season. Although it has been busy all through October, this is when the mill gets terribly busy." Sally told them. "I really love this time of year. It is what the enchanted mill is all about. You will love going through the portal to the North Pole."

"You actually went through the portal to the North Pole?" Cathy was in awe.

"Of course, many times. It is the best perk of all jobs." Sally laughed and smiled as she reminisced.

"I can't wait to step through the Portal's purple swirling mass," Cathy replied. "What is it like stepping through?"

"It is similar to witch flight. Nothing to be afraid of. Well except, it has been Adam that has gone through with me in recent years. But that would be a bit awkward and not wise at the moment." Sally pondered, "I can't go with you, as I am a ghost."

"Who else could go with me, I don't want to go on my own." Cathy was getting a little worried.

"You could take Ulysses. You could go flying with him, in his dragon form. That is a very fond memory of mine, flying with the dragon." Sally smiled. "Flying among the Northern Lights is something to experience more than once."

"You flew with a dragon? What did you shift into?" Cathy gasped.

"Just a small purple dragon, of course. What else would you shift into to fly with a dragon?" Sally teased.

"Well, that I remain to see for myself. But I have always wanted to see the Northern Lights." Cathy was thinking of how she could shift into a dragon too.

"I can assure you, you will see the lights, when you go through the portal." Sally grinned. "But now we must get down to the cellar. The others will be waiting for us. Don't look so concerned.

Brian is standing in for Adam, today. Harold, Roger, and Uncle John will also be there. They are your official guardians."

"I am ready, I have kept up with all my lessons. Now the time is here to put everything into practice. "Cathy stood up to leave.

"Are you coming down, my way Tiddles?" Oskar teased. Referring to Cathy's first attempt at shapeshifting and ended up as a glossy black cat.

"Sorry, Fluffy. Today I shall go down the human witchy way. Not as Tiddles." She laughed as she tickled Oskar/Fluffy behind his ears.

"Suit yourself, I am off to round up the other familiars. See you in the cellar," and he disappeared.

"Shall we walk down, via the corridors. I want to conserve as much energy as possible." Cathy asked the two ghosts. "Will I be able to go into the cellar?" asked Clara Jane.

"You mean to say, you have never been into the cellar?" Sally asked.

Blushing, Clara Jane gave herself away. "Well, I might have visited Ulysses a few times with Pearl and Ruby. But I promise, we never came in the Santa Season. We didn't dare to."

"Of course, you can come today." Sally reassured her. "You are part of the family now."

Tears appeared in Clara Jane's eyes. "I can never thank you enough for all that you have done for me and my family," She wept.

"Shall we get moving, and not sentimental?" Cathy interrupted,

"Sure, follow me and we will collect Harold on the way." Sally led them through the door into the secret corridor. Harold and Roger were both waiting, near his apartment. "Cathy how are you feeling today?" Harold asked.

"Good morning gentlemen. I am feeling fine. I didn't have too much of the mulled cider last night. So, I could keep a clear head for today."

The group of witches, wizards and ghosts made their way through the maze of corridors to the door leading into the cellar. When they arrived, they found a few of the old coven members waiting, along with Uncle John and Margaret. It made Cathy smile to see her Uncle, now happily having time with Margaret.

Once Cathy had found out her ancestry, he had relaxed so much and was a different person. Betty and Desdemona were also waiting by the cellar door. Brian and Stephen appeared in the corridor.

"Good Morning everyone." Harold greeted the small group of people. "Today is an important day for Cathy and Riverside Mill. Today we open the portal and start the final run up to Christmas process. Toys and presents are sent through the portal, and on Christmas Eve Sants uses the portal for his UK deliveries."

Everyone clapped and cheered. Cathy felt a bit unsure; she was the only one that hadn't done this before, and it all was up to her to open the portal.

"Today the mill begins the process of Santa Season, that was set in place by the Buckley family, many years ago. The warehouse and the units, will now step up a gear to deliver the correct goods at the correct time." he continued.

"Cathy, can you please lead the way, and open the door for us?" Roger asked her.

Cathy placed her hand on the cellar door handle. This was the first time she had actually gone into the cellar through the door, her previous visits had been by witch flight or as Tiddles.

"Everyone is so excited," she thought to herself. The warmth of the magic spread through her and the door handle. She could feel her own magic growing in strength. The door opened and the steps lit up, so Cathy made her way down them and into the cellar.

At the bottom of the steps, Ulysses was waiting for them. "Miss Catherine, welcome to the cellar. I am looking forward to handing over the portal for your keeping." He bowed low to Cathy, as he spoke to her.

"Yikes, all my responsibility," she thought. "Good morning, Ulysses, please can you lead the way to the portal."

The group walked through the cellar, unit they were in front of the security door that led to the portal. Cathy was surprised to see some chairs set out in front of the door.

"Do not panic," Sally whispered, as she saw Cathy look bewildered. "You don't have to make a big speech. Just remember the words you have been learning."

Cathy saw the group of familiars sat to the side of the chairs. Oskar, Hamish, Nalah, Marley, and Margaret's owl – Hawkeye. They all looked serious, as they waited for the ceremony to start.

"*Deep breaths*," Cathy told herself. Lucky for Cathy, Harold stood up to start the proceedings.

"Ladies, Gentlemen and Familiars. Welcome to the annual Opening of the Portal Ceremony. This, as we all know, will be the first of many for Catherine. This is a huge honour for the community and the Mill, to hold the Northwest Portal for the North Pole here. Cathy, please proceed." Harold said.

"*Here we go*," Cathy thought as she stood to join Harold. "Thank you everyone for being here today, to support me during my very first Opening of the Portal ceremony. I will be honest and let you all know I am nervous. Harold, do you have the ceremonial robes?"

Harold got the robe, off a nearby table, and helped Cathy put it on.

"Right, here we go," she told the anticipating audience. She saw her Grandma give her a thumbs up signal. An overly excite Clara Jane stood next to Sally. "First of all, Ulysses, could you please open the first security door for me."

Ulysses stepped forward and keyed the numbers into the keypad. The first door swung open and then Cathy and the others, made their way up the ramp into the secure unit. In front of them was the glowing doorway. An arched doorway, that was filled with a purple swirling mist.

Sally nudged Cathy forward, "it is all yours Cathy. Remember the lines and all will be well. I always loved this part of the proceedings."

Cathy took a deep breath and started her well-rehearsed lines. "We are here in front of the portal. From the Opening of the Portal, Christmas at Riverside Mill will begin."

Cathy lifted her gown up and moved directly in front of the portal. She moved her hands out in front, like she had practised, both arms stretched out in front of her. The words she had rehearsed over and over, formed in her mind.

"I will being the process now, if you could all form a semicircle around me, please?" She asked the group. The room hushed, as everyone moved into place behind Cathy, even the familiars stood in the semi-circle.

*"Right, here I go, oh for Adam to be with me, "*she thought. *"He was my main support throughout all the learning."*

Cathy closed her eyes and began to chant the words. Her whole body took on an unusual feeling as she recited the words. Silence descended on the room, everyone was watching Cathy or the portal. Sally watched on with pride, as she listened to Cathy say the words, exactly as she should. Cathy herself, felt the power of her magic flow through her arms towards the portal.

After what felt like hours, Cathy finished the spell and stepped back, and slowly opened her eyes. She looked at the portal. It didn't look any different than before.

"What is supposed to happen?" she asked Sally. She had been expecting fireworks and a grand opening.

"The portal hasn't opened," gasped Harold.

"But Cathy did everything correctly," Sally replied. "Something is amiss. The portal has not opened like it should do."

"What can I do?" panic set in for Cathy. "Have I done it wrong?"

"Not at all Cathy," Harold assured her. "Ulysses, can you round up the troops, to put the security in place please?"

Ulysses nodded and took out, what looked to be a very old-fashioned mobile phone. He prodded a few numbers in and smiled back at Harold. "Give them a few minutes and they will be here Mr Harold."

"We now need the vampires and their experience." Sally told Cathy. "They helped to create the portal. We desperately need them to come out into the sunlight now."

Ulysses excused himself from the portal area and went back out down the ramp. Within minutes he was back with five colleagues. They all looked the same, short and in armour.

"Excellent," Harold said, "Guards, you are needed to protect the portal, until we can get it fixed. If you need anything, please tell Ulysses to contact me. We all thank you for your time."

The five men and Ulysses nodded to Harold and bowed to Cathy. They took up their positions in front of the portal.

"Rest assured Miss Cathy, no one will touch the portal." Ulysses told her.

Harold led them all back down the ramp, and through the key padded door, closing it behind him.

"What just happened?" Cathy asked.

"The portal is stuck. It happened a few decades ago. Do you remember Sally?" Harold smiled at Sally.

"Oh yes, we thought it was broken. But we nearly killed the vampire boys getting them to fix it. Don't worry Cathy, we had better get on our way to Ashway Towers, before we lose any more time. Harold, can you phone them, and run Cathy around please. I will meet you there." Sally said.

Chapter 11

Return to the Vampire's Lair

Before Cathy knew what was happening, she was whisked off in Harold's car, and on her way to visit the vampires.

"I have spoken with Albers," Roger told them. "he will inform the brothers, and they will be ready for us, when we arrive."

"I feel all in a whirl," Cathy admitted. "I grabbed the grimoire and the crystals I have been working with, I hope they can help."

The car travelled up the hill out of Green Valley. Before long, they approached the turn off, that would lead them down into the valley at the furthest end of the Dove Stone Lake.

When they approached the main door of Ashway Towers, Cathy saw that Albers was stood outside waiting for them. The three vampire brothers were stood in the shade, in the shadows of the doorway.

They were led back into the huge lounge. Worried looks were on everyone's faces. Harold told them what was – or wasn't happening with the portal. Sally also arrived in the room soon after.

"So, what can we do?" Cathy asked the assembled group.

"We need to fix two situations now," Tomasz told them. "We need to go and visit the portal to see what the problem is. But that needs to be done in daylight hours. For that to happen, we need the ability to go outside and not frizzle. How are you doing with your experiment Fillipe?"

"I am nearly ready to try it out, I just need Cathy's magic." Fillipe replied.

"I think I might have the answer." Cathy told them, "I saw a citrine flashing in the shop lighting the other day, so I have been experimenting too. I have been looking at both citrine and moonstone. The citrine for the sunshine and the moonstone for nighttime. I have brought some samples with me if you want to take a look."

Reaching into her bag, Cathy brought out a small box of various packages. "I have some ground up some of the crystals, and I have also cut slivers. I wasn't sure how it would work with the silicon chip."

She passed the samples over to Fillipe and continued. "I have researched in my family grimoire. I am reasonably sure I have the correct spell to use with it. Although, I thought I had the correct spell for the Opening of The Portal ceremony too." Cathy sighed, as she thought her magic was failing her.

"Cathy," Sally told her, "It is not your magic, the portal has just got a glitch in the system. It has happened before; it will be fixed. The grimoire only shows you the correct spells."

Fillipe took hold of the samples, "Cathy, these are amazing. This looks just what we need. Shall we head to my lab and try them, whilst the others work out what the portal problem could be?"

"That sounds a good idea," Dumar laughed, "you two go and have fun, we will see if we can come up with any ideas."

Cathy followed Fillipe down the long mahogany clad corridors, toward the back of the house. She could hear Franziska telling the young boys to calm down. *"Word must have got out about our visit."* Cathy smiled, *"I do hope this works."*

She followed Fillipe into his laboratory, it was so much like her own Temple Room.

"Look at this Cathy," Fillipe showed her a sample of the silicon chip he had been working on. "This is where the crystal needs to be. It is exceedingly small, but I am sure the crystals will be enough, along with your magic."

"That is so small. Are you sure it will work?" Cathy asked.

"The chip needs to be small, it will be inserted at the top of our arm, more or less on the shoulder. We need to protect our whole bodies from the sunlight. A slice of each crystal bound together with the ground up crystals, and my technology should be enough." Fillipe was practically jumping around with excitement.

"Shall we try it?" He asked Cathy.

"What now? Today," Cathy panicked.

"No time like the present, we have the technology, the crystals, and your magic. It will take a few attempts to perfect it. But I am willing to try today if you are willing?" Fillipe laughed at Cathy's panicked face. "Your magic is the best, stop worrying."

"Gosh, sure if you are game." Cathy said, while thinking to herself, *"if he wasn't a vampire, he would make superb boyfriend material."* She felt herself blushing at her own thoughts.

"I will break down the crystals and add them to the chip. Take a seat and you can watch me working. When I think I am ready, I will ask for your magic." Fillipe smiled at her, as he got down to his work.

Cathy was a little worried about her magic, what if she didn't get it right, and he sizzled in front of her. She didn't want to be responsible for the death of a vampire.

"Don't look so worried, Cathy. I will know more or less right away if the chip is working. I won't turn into dust in front of you. We can already, step outside in the sunlight, for a minute or so. We just chose not to at the moment." Fillipe laughed as her face relaxed from worry to the interest in his creation.

"I do hope so," Cathy replied and relaxed. She watched him work with the tiniest of materials, mainly under a microscope.

After what felt like hours, Fillipe stood up, and turned to face Cathy. "Now, it is time for your magic Cathy."

Cathy moved to the bench, in front of her was a tiny silicon chip. Not much bigger than a small fingernail.

Concentrating, she was glad she had brought her grimoire with her. Holding the book tight, she closed her eyes and felt the magic start to pulse through her body. She held the silicon chip in her spare hand. The magic flowed from the grimoire, through her body and into the tiny piece of technology.

Eventually, she opened her eyes, and saw Fillipe staring at her.

"I actually saw the magic, transferring from you into the chip. There was a gold glow coming from your hand." He told her, in awe of hr magic.

"I felt it too," Cathy laughed. "Now what?"

"I will implant it in my arm. Look away now if you are squeamish." Fillipe started to remove his jacket and unbutton his crisp white shirt. Instead of looking away, Cathy was transfixed on watching the vampire disrobe in front of her.

Fillipe took a small scalpel and made a slight cut in the top of his arm, almost on the shoulder. Cathy passed him the magical chip. When they touched, the magic passed between them too.

"Wow, you are powerful," he teased her, as he slipped the chip in place under his skin. "I felt the surge of magic, when you touched me."

Cathy blushed, "Well, I am not sure what to say now." They both laughed as the electricity between them sparked.

Fillipe put a small stick-on stitch in the cut, to keep the chip in place. To Cathy' s dismay, he then put his shirt back on.

"Let me top up the magic, now it is in place," Cathy placed both her hands directly onto his arm and recited the spell again.

"Ready?" Fillipe asked, "shall we go and tell the others?"

"Only if you are 100% ready." Cathy worried face came back.

"How can you worry with that powerful magic. Come on," Fillipe laughed has he held her hand and they made their way back to the lounge, where the others were waiting.

A group of expectant faces were watching them, as they walked into the room.

"Shall we go outside?" Fillipe asked. He took Cathy's hand again, as they made their way to the front door. The others followed behind in disbelief. Decades of trying various experiments had always ended in failure and disappointment.

Fillipe walked to the huge front door, and Albers stood and opened it for him to go outside.

Cathy crossed her fingers and toes, hoping her magic was just what they needed.

Fillipe walked outside into the late afternoons autumnal sunshine. Cathy, and the others all held their breath. Fillipe walked around the car park, as they all watched on.

Tiny footsteps clattered through the main entrance hall towards the door. "I am so sorry," Franziska apologised. "I couldn't keep them away, how long has he been outside?"

Mikael and Izaac pushed through the crowd, until Dumar held them back. "Not yet boys, Uncle Fillipe is just testing. He has been out about five minutes or so. Boys this could be an especially important day in our lives as vampires. Watch and listen to all that is happening."

"Miss Cathy," Mikael whispered, "Have you made this with magic?"

"I do hope so," smiled Cathy. She suddenly realised how much this meant for them all.

"So do I Miss Cathy, I want to play cricket and football. I bet it is much better than playing down in the cellar." Mikael sighed, as the outdoors were still out of reach, for now.

After about ten minutes, Fillipe came back into the building. "How was it, what did it feel like?" Questions from everyone.

"I cannot tell you how it felt." He said the expectant group. "I am still here and not fried like Cathy thought I would be. I think with a few tweaks, and more of Cathy's incredible magic. Yes, I think we will all be playing cricket and football outside.

" Yippee," shouted the two young vampires. They then proceeded to run rings around the massive table in the centre of the entrance hall.

Dumar, Tomasz and Fillipe hugged each other, and dragged Cathy and Franziska into the group hug too. *Phew, vampires have testosterone too."* Cathy thought.

"Thank you, Cathy," the three brothers all said at once.

"If you let me have a couple of days to make the tweaks, then we can have another go. If all is working, we can then come to the mill, to fix the portal. We have come up with a few ideas of what may be the problem." Tomasz told her.

"Would you be able to come back, as soon as we are ready, to work your magic again?" Fillipe asked her, with a twinkle in his eye, which wasn't missed by any of the others.

"Of course. I will bring further crystals, and the grimoire. I will get plenty of rest and recharge my batteries. Just to be sure I have enough for you all." Cathy smiled.

"Oh, Cathy, there is absolutely nothing wrong with your magic," Fillipe teased her.

Harold saw Cathy looking a bit embarrassed and rescued her. "I think it is time we took our leave, and I got Cathy home for the said rest. Two big surges of her power today. must make her feel drained. The Portal and the Silicon Chip. No matter how good she is, it isn't a never-ending supply."

"Thank you, Cathy," Sally smiled and hugged her granddaughter. "See you back at the mill."

When Cathy turned to leave the house, Izaac and Mikael ran over to her. "Miss Cathy, will you play cricket and football with us outside too?" Their two expectant faces looked up at her.

"Of course, I will, and you can maybe come to the mill and meet Neil and Nick, they live there now. You could all play together." Cathy just loved these two young boys, even if they were vampires.

On the short journey back to the mill, Cathy listened to Harold and Roger chatting about the day's events. She felt herself lulled into sleep as the motion of the car rocked her into a deep slumber.

She woke with a start when the car stopped outside the entrance to her apartment. Waiting outside the entrance was Adam. He had a concerned look on his face.

"I heard there was a problem with the portal?" he asked Cathy.

"Yes, we have a problem. The portal didn't open. But the vampires will be able to come and fix it in the next couple of days." Cathy replied. Was it the vampire magic, or just the fact Adam didn't seem to be putting up much of a fight to get rid of Tamara? But Cathy just didn't feel like talking to him.

"I am very tired," she told him, "I will see you around with your wife." She let herself into the corridor and walked to the apartment, alone. She let herself in, and she heard Sally telling Adam to leave her alone and give Cathy time. Her magic was blossoming, and she was coming into the powerful witch that she was. She then told him to sort his own life out, before pestering Cathy.

Cathy smiled as she listened to what her Grandma was saying and walked straight to her bedroom. Magicked on her pyjamas and climbed straight into bed, to dream of portals and vampires.

Chapter 12

The Northwest Coven Leaders

The leaders of the main Northwest Covens sat around the table in the boardroom. Cathy had organised an emergency meeting, to update them on the problems with the portal. Margaret had sent the invitations using Hawkeye, her owl familiar. The acceptance replies had comeback immediately.

Alongside Cathy, sat Glynis and Bronwen. They had appointed themselves her deputies. Cathy introduced herself and apologised for the hastily arranged first meeting. No one seemed to mind, everyone was pleased to finally meet Cathy and to visit the Enchanted Mill.

Cathy told them all about the failed attempt at opening the Portal. The impact this would affect all the covens, with this being the only portal in the Northwest.

"How are the experiments with your vampires progressing?" Monika, from the Manchester and Salford coven.

"Exciting. They are just tweaking the silicon chip. I was there the other day with Fillipe when he tested the first prototype." Cathy told them.

"Are your vampires sexy. Like ours?" giggled Sammy from the Chester coven.

"It is such a shame we cannot photograph them," laughed Jeanette from the Lancaster coven. "They don't show up on photos, such a pity."

"Do we all have vampires?" Cathy asked them.

"Of course, we do, vampires, shifters, witches, and wizards and so on. We all have our magical communities. In one way or another, we are all linked back to your family." Jeannette replied.

"I have so much to learn." Cathy sighed.

"Oh Cathy, stop that self-doubt." Sammy told her. "We have all heard of the marvellous things that you have already accomplished."

"We are all taking over from our grandmothers. We all have to learn together," Andrea from the Liverpool coven told her. "Some of our grandmothers have passed like yours, and some are just teaching the ropes for when they too pass over."

"Back to the vampires, yes, they are extremely sexy men. Too much at times." Cathy brought them up to date about the three brothers, "But Mikael and Izaac are gorgeous, to die for. Whoops, I don't mean that literally. Gosh we are talking about vampires!!"

"Oh my, that is a good one," laughed Glynis. "To die for a young vampire!"

The whole group had a good laugh and Cathy smiled to herself, as she saw the group of strangers turning into good friends.

"Would you all like to go and see the cellar and the portal. We could try combining our powers to see if we can identify the problem?" Cathy asked the group.

"Absolutely!" Monika stood up. "Come on ladies, wait till we tell our grans that we have actually seen the portal."

The coven of witches, led by Harold, of course, (He didn't miss out on anything,) made their way through the mill to the cellar door.

"What a wonderful feeling this mill has," commented Olwyn from the Liverpool coven.

"Our coven headquarters is quite boring compared to this mill," moaned Lisa from the Carlisle coven.

"Nonsense, you are all living in the grounds of Hadrian's Wall." Monika laughed.

"You live on a roman wall?" Glynis joined the conversation. "We have a small Roman Fortlet at Castleshaw, on the outer edge of Upper Valley."

"I love Roman history," Cathy commented.

"You will have to ask Peter to run an archaeological dig at the fort," Glynis suggested.

"That is a very good idea," Cathy laughed. "Do you think there will be any ghosts?"

"None that we have seen in the past, but please feel free to come and have a look." Glynis said.

"Feel free to come and visit us too, Hadrian's Wall and the Roman forts will be a great adventure for you," Lisa told her. "A tour of all the northwest covens after the Santa Season."

"Now, I do like that idea." Cathy laughed, "A few days on a tour sounds good to me."

"Ladies, if I may interrupt, we are at the entrance to the cellar. Cathy, could you please do the honours and open the door?" Harold asked.

Cathy placed her hand on the door handle and the door automatically opened before her. She led the group down the steps into the underground room. When they reached the bottom of the steps, Ulysses was waiting for them.

"Miss Cathy is everything all right? We, didn't expect you today." He asked with a panic expression on his face.

"Everything is fine, I am just going to show my fellow northwest coven leaders the portal. We are going to try to combine our magic and see if we can do anything with the portal. It was just an idea while we are all together." Cathy told him. "The vampires are on the edge of a breakthrough, so they should be here any day soon."

"Thank you, Miss Cathy, I will lead the way to the portal." Ulysses led them through the very bright cellar to the secure door.

The women and Harold followed him. The stocky guard led them through the secure door and up the ramp to the portal.

"Wow, this is incredible," one of the witches cried.

"Look at the portal, it is everything I have been told about in our lessons," another said.

"You have lessons about the portal?" Cathy asked them.

"Yes, we have lessons on lots of things, but the Christmas portal is so special." Lisa told her.

"It is a pity it doesn't work yet," Cathy sighed.

"It will do soon. What I would give for a walk through that purple mist." Lisa told her. "You are so lucky Cathy."

"I don't feel so at the moment." Cathy admitted. She didn't want to mention Adam and Tamara, so she blamed her feelings on the portal problems.

"Shall we stand in a semi-circle and try to spell the portal into working?" Cathy suggested.

Ulysess ordered the five guards to stand down, whilst Cathy and her guests prepared the area in front of the portal, to get ready for the spell work. Cathy looked at the five guards and realised that she hadn't been introduced to them properly. When the portal hadn't opened, she had been whisked off to the vampire house. She walked over to Ulysess and asked if it would be possible for her to come back and be introduced properly. Ulysess face beamed as he nodded in agreement.

"Certainly, Miss Cathy, anytime. It will be our pleasure." Ulysess bowed at Cathy as he walked back to the guards.

Cathy finished preparing the area in front of the portal. Candles were lit, and a chalked pentacle were in place.

Cathy led with the spell she had used for the original opening ceremony, repeating the chant as previously used. The others joined in with her, and the purple mist began to swirl.

The group all repeated the words, along with Cathy. There was a visible shift in the energy of the room. But after ten minutes or so, Cathy told them to stop.

"We are not getting anywhere, it must be a mechanical fault, that only the vampires can fix," she told them.

Sadly, the women stepped back from the semi-circle, and the guards swiftly took their places back in front of the opening.

"Shall we go back to the boardroom and have some refreshments? We can chat in there and ponder our vampires," Cathy asked them.

"Yes, I don't think we can help with the portal," Monika smiled at Cathy. "I think a chat about our various vampires would help us all."

"I will leave you ladies to your chat and have a quick check on the rest of the mill," Harold said, slightly embarrassed about vampire chat.

On leaving the cellar, Cathy told Ulysses she would be back when her guests had departed.

"Thank you, Miss Cathy, we will await your visit," Ulysess said as he bowed again.

The young women made their way back through the mill to find a buffet waiting for them. Kim and Wendy had used their particular magic again.

Cathy learnt so much from the other young coven leaders. She planned to visit them all the following spring, when the winter had passed, and the weather would improve. Even though the portal still didn't open, she felt she had gained another new set of friends.

Chapter 13

The Cellar Dwellers Friends

When the guests had returned, via witch flight to their own covens, Cathy made her way back down to the cellar. She was feeling disappointed that the collective attempt to open the portal had failed. Cathy just felt like sitting down and pondering about her life. She thought often of Adam but had a feeling he was taking to life as a father.

Letting herself back through the cellar door, Cathy called out to Ulysses, to make him aware that she had returned. Ulysses met her as she walked towards the portal door.

"Miss Cathy," he greeted her. "You look so sad. The portal will be working again soon."

"I know, I just feel at a loss. The portal won't open. Adam is playing happy families." Cathy sighed.

"Miss Cathy, come and meet my family. The lads haven't been formerly introduced to you yet." Ulysess tapped the keypad to the door to the portal and led her up the ramp.

"Stand down lads get the chairs and table. Miss Cathy is feeling despondent." Ulysess commanded. "Miss Cathy, let me introduce you to my cousins. They are all goblins, I was the only one turned into a boggart, by your ancestors. The others soon learnt by my mistake."

Cathy saw the five goblins move quickly in front of her, soon a small table and six chairs had been set up in front of the portal. A coffee mug and cups set upon it, in front of her.

"Come and sit with us Miss Cathy," Ulysses gestured to a chair. "Let me introduce my cousins, Gordo, Grengo, Gergo, Glenk and Gloof. Our mothers were sisters."

"Pleased to meet you all." Cathy smiled, as she shook each of their hands. "Are you all as old as Ulysess? Where do you live?"

"One question at once, Miss, please." Gordo stood up tall. "I am the oldest of us all, My name is Gordo. Miss Cathy, it our honour to make your acquaintance. To answer your questions, yes, we are all as old as Ulysess, some of us older. Secondly, we live on the top of the hill, known these days as Pots and Pans. We have a cave near the old druid stone, that was the origin of the pots and pans legend, because of the hollows in the rock."

"We haven't always lived there Miss," interrupted the smallest of the goblins. "We used to live on the hillside that is now under the railway track. We had the most impressive cave system on that hillside. But in the 1840s, the railway line was started, and for our own safety we were moved to our present location.

"Gloof, have you quite finished interrupting?" Gordo asked.

The small goblin blushed as he was reprimanded.

"Sorry Gordo and Miss Cathy." Gloof muttered.

"Have you ever noticed the house on the bend to the station brew?" Grengo asked Cathy.

"Yes, the small pointy one, right on the bend?" Cathy replied.

"That is the correct one, If you look carefully, just above the doorway, is has a sign for 'Goblin Manor,' That was in our honour, as the whole railway line covered our dwellings. The villagers at the time were used to mixing with us. After Ulysess was turned into a boggart and imprisoned in the dungeon, we all changed our mischievous habits," Grengo told her.

"I took one for the whole family," Ulysess grunted. "But I will admit that it has worked out well for my whole family. Since your ancestors took us under your care, we have been indebted to you all."

"Yes, Miss Cathy, when the railway started to be constructed, the navvies came back again. But they were not like the canal navvies in the early 1800s. They were niece fellas and we all got along and worked together. The railway lot were different, they ridiculed our work and made us uncomfortable. That was when your ancestor saw our discomfort and created the new dwelling place," Gordo continued. "We help Alf and Eric help to protect the valleys. Normally we are not in view. We are on call for when we are needed, such as the portal problems."

"I do appreciate all your help, all of you." Cathy told them. She was fascinated that the area she loved so much, had so many individual characters. "Tell me more about your lives, it must have been very interesting living so long and seeing the area change so much."

Cathy listened as Ulysess and his goblin cousins talked to her, for what seemed to be hours. They had their own community up on the top of Alderman hill, near the Pots and Pans stone.

"When the war memorial was built in the early 1920s, we were an integral part of the construction. The villagers asked us to help, because of our strength. Because of our connection with your ancestors, we have helped a lot of the construction in the area." Gordo explained.

"We also helped with the building of the top reservoir, Chew Reservoir." Gloof chipped in. "Did you know there is still the outline of the old railway track that used to take the stone to the construction site?"

"I had no idea there was ever a railway to the Top reservoir, or Chew reservoir as it is called," Cathy was learning new things about the area each day.

"You can still make out the line of the trackway on the hillside," Gloof told her. "Look out for it when you fly over again."

"You have seen me flying?" Cathy asked.

"Of course, Sally often stops by our homestead to tell us about your progress." Gordo laughed. "In fact, you must visit soon and bring Ulysess with you, after the Santa Season rush."

"I think that would be a wonderful treat for Ulysess, but after the Closing of the Portal Ceremony." Cathy agreed and smiled as she saw Ulysess looking so excited.

"When did you last go home Ulysess," she asked him.

"Miss Sally always lets me visit once a month. One of these lads always takes my place, so the portal is never left unguarded." He bowed as he finished speaking to her.

"Then we shall keep that arrangement." Cathy beamed. Her group of goblin security and construction men may be useful in the future. But she would like a look deeper into the Pots and Pans legend, and their homestead.

Cathy sat listening to the small group, enthralled with their tales and stories. But out of the blue Sally appear before them.

"Cathy, we have been looking all over for you. We couldn't find you." She began to say.

"What is it Grandma, I thought you could telepath to communicate with me." Cathy asked anxiously.

"Tomasz rang, can you get round to the Towers as soon as possible? Take the supplies of citrine and moonstone too. Don't forget to take your grimoire too," Sally told her, hurriedly. "They are on the edge of the breakthrough."

"Miss Cathy," Ulysses bowed. "We have had the pleasure of your company, and we do hope we can continue our conversation in the near future. But please rush and help the vampires with the breakthrough they need. Santa Season does really need to begin."

"Thank you everyone," Cathy and Sally took a quick witch flight back to her apartment.

Chapter 14

Spells and Silicon

Gillian and Clara Jane were working together, making more sets of jewellery for the shop or online sales.

"Whoa, what is the hurry?" Gillian asked when Cathy suddenly appeared before her.

"We need the new citrine and moonstone supplies. The vampires are on the verge of a breakthrough." Cathy brought them up to date on the news, as quickly as she could.

"Gran, can you get Harold, Betty, and Desdemona. I will ask Uncle John and Margaret to come along with us." Cathy asked. "We should have enough magic energy for the spell work."

"Cathy, it is already late afternoon and going dark." Sally reminded her. "it could be an exceptionally long night of working. You and I can go now, and the rest can come round in the morning, perhaps at dawn. Harold will organise everything at this end."

"Ok," Cathy replied, her brain was working too quick.

"Get the crystals that you will need and then we can get going." Sally told her.

Gillian helped Cathy to securely pack the crystals and her grimoire, safety inside a rucksack. She was going to use witch flight, so the rucksack would be easier to carry.

"Good luck." She whispered to Cathy.

"Thanks," Cathy whispered back.

Using her ability to take witch flight, Cathy found herself in the huge reception hall of Ashway Towers. Albers was waiting for her, alongside her Grandma Sally.

"Welcome Miss Cathy," Albers greeted her. "The Masters are waiting for you in the lab. Would you let me carry your rucksack, it looks heavy?"

Taking off her rucksack and gaining her balance after the witch flight, Cathy followed Albers through the long corridor to the lab at the back of the building. When Cathy walked into Fillipe's laboratory, she felt the same rush of magic and power, that she felt in her own Temple Room.

"*They must be connected*," she thought to herself.

A stampede of tiny feet shook her from her thoughts.

"Miss Cathy," an excited Izaac shouted, while he flung himself around her legs and waist.

"Hello young men," she said to the pair of young, excited vampires.

"Have you brought further supplies Miss Cathy," Mikael asked. "Uncle Fillipe has used all the ones you brought before. Please come and see them." Mikael led Cathy and Sally towards the experimental area of the lab. Cathy saw their father and two uncles looking busy and profoundly serious.

"Boys, what have I told you about running about, especially in Uncle Fillipe's lab." Dumar chastised his sons.

"But father, Miss Cathy is here, at last." Izaac answered his father, while using his big black eyes to plead with him.

"Cathy, welcome back," Dumar greeted her.

"I don't feel like I have been away. I was at the portal with Ulysess and his cousins. They were telling me about their lives." Cathy explained.

"Oh yes, the five brothers. Brilliant workers." Dumar agreed and led Cathy to his two vampire brothers.

"Hi Cathy," Fillipe turned to greet her, taking off his protective glasses. "I am so pleased to see you this evening. I see you have brought the supplies. Let me show you the adjustments we have made."

"He hasn't stopped working since you left," Tomasz laughed. "It is a good job vampires don't need to sleep."

Fillipe began to tell Cathy all that he had done, since her last visit. Tweaking this and that.

"I am so nearly there; I have been outside in the winter sunshine a few times today and felt fine. But I am out of citrine, and of course, your magic." He was so charming.

Tomasz and Dumar coughed to remind him they were both still in the room, and they caught Cathy blushing again.

"Have you eaten Cathy," Tomasz asked.

"I had lunch with the other leaders of the northwest covens. We also tried to combine our magic at portal, but to no avail." Cathy told him.

"I shall go and ask Albers to organise dinner, for in an hour or so," Tomasz turned to leave the room. "Cathy, I hope you are prepared for a long night ahead."

"Yes, my grandma told me to prepare for a long night ahead. But Harold and some of the coven members will be arriving at dawn, to lend me a hand with the magic." Cathy replied.

"Excellent," Tomasz smiled. "Izaak and Mikael, stay at your bench and finish your lessons. You can stay in Uncle Fillipe's lab, only if you behave yourselves."

"Yes, Uncle Tomasz," they said together.

Cathy smiled at the young vampires. *"Tomorrow could be the first time they go out in sunlight. How incredible must that be to them* all." Cathy thought. *"To never have to worry about the sunshine again. This is more than just a major breakthrough; it is a life changer."*

Very soon, the room became incredibly quiet, with everyone getting organised. Cathy unpacked her rucksack. Fillipe inspected all the new crystals.

"This is a fine selection, Cathy. You have done well." Fillipe smiled at Cathy.

"What can we do to help?" Dumar asked.

"Can one of you slice the moonstone, as thinly as possible please. And someone do the same with the citrine," Fillipe instructed. "Cathy, can you help me make the tiny speck that we will need for the silicon chips."

Sally sat with the young vampires and helped to keep their minds on their lessons, while everyone got on with the tasks allocated to them. The hours passed quickly; dinner was served. Franziska tried to get the young boys to go to bed but failed miserably. They were not going to miss out on this exciting time. Eventually she gave in and sat beside them In the laboratory.

The three vampires and Cathy worked tirelessly. At various times, the brothers would leave the lab. Cathy could only assume they had gone for their own version of a strong coffee, like she was drinking constantly.

The evening turned into nighttime, and eventually the early hours, turned into dawn.

Albers brought Harold and the other coven members to the lab.

"Good morning, everyone," Fillipe greeted them all. Some of the witches, including Gillian, had never met the vampires before and appeared to be in a trancelike state.

"Morning," Cathy laughed, "perfect timing, we have worked through the night. The crystals are all in place. We just need the combined magic to seal the process. Them Fillipe and Tomasz will venture outside, to watch the sunrise. For now, Dumar and his family will stay in the shade, should anything untoward happen."

Everyone gasped at the idea of anything untoward happening.

"I think we will be fine, if only for a few minutes," Fillipe reassured everyone.

"It must be noted," Cathy became serious. "The magic we will be using to bond the crystals and the silicon chip, will hold a clause that if a vampire wearing said chip, does not follow the rules, the chip will allow a certain time limit for the wearer to get back indoors, if out in daylight."

"You have thought of everything," Harold beamed like a proud grandfather.

"This is an historic moment for the vampire community, we have to protect everyone in the process." Dumar told the group. "Not all vampires are as well trained as our family. Once word gets out what we have done. They will be trying to copy them. But Cathy's magic is quite unique, so it should not be easy to copy."

"Phew," Cathy heard a few of the older witches sighing.

"Everyone, if we could make our way to the makeshift altar. The chips are laid out and are all completed, except for the combined magic." Cathy led the way. "All we need now is a final blast of our combined magic."

The small group walked the length of the lab, Cathy could tell that many where in awe of the actual room and the event of the day.

"Please form a semi-circle. Fillipe, Tomas, Dumar and family, please step inside the semi-circle." Cathy instructed. She held her hands with next person, and soon they were all holding hands.

Cathy watch Izaac and Mikael, she had not seen them this quiet before. They looked petrified in the centre of the old witches. Cathy smiled at them and let them know they were safe.

"I will start the spell work, if you could end the chant with, 'so mote it be,' after each line." Cathy continued.

Cathy had rehearsed these lines, from her grimoire, so many times before. She knew them word perfect. But she still had hold of her trusty grimoire. The witches and wizards stood around the vampires and the altar with the chips laid out, Their voices tuned in together, to sound like one voice.

Then the time arrived for the vampires to insert their chips into their arms. Albers led Harold and the other witches back to the lounge to give the vampires some privacy.

"Shall we insert ours too?" Dumar asked.

"I don't see why not. If ours work, I can't imagine you wanting to wait for long to join us." Fillipe laughed. "Nor will they." The two boys had already taken their tops off and were offering their arms for their chip to be implanted,

Cathy helped them all to select their own chip. Adding a final blast of her magic as it was slipped under the skin of each vampire.

"Shall we go?" Fillipe asked, when everyone was chipped, and they had dressed in their usual smart suits.

"I am ready," Tomasz replied.

"So are we," Dumar said whilst he held the hands of his two young sons, Izaac in turn held his mother's hand too. Franziska was noticeably quiet. Duma gently leaned over and kissed her. "This time, it will work. We will be free."

She relaxed and nodded. "We have tried so many times, why will this time be different?"

"We have Cathy's magic and Fillipe's technology. Come along." He gently led the family after the others towards the main door.

They arrived at the front of the house and were soon met by the other witches and wizards.

"Cathy," Fillipe asked her, "Would you accompany me to see the sunrise?"

Taking hold of his cool hand, Cathy felt a surge of power course through her. "Of course, Fillipe, shall we?"

The couple walked through the door of the mansion; Albers bowed to his master as he held the door. The couple walked across the car park area and towards the garden. A small bench had been built that overlooked the whole of Green Valley.

Tomasz walked alongside and the three sat down on the bench, with Cathy in the middle. Slowly the sun began to rise from behind the hillside opposite them.

"How do both feel?" She asked nervously.

"So far so good," Fillipe smiled at her.

"I feel amazing, this is my first time outside in the daylight," admitted Tomasz. "Fillipe was always the one to do the testing."

Without warning Dumar and the boys were stood alongside them. "We couldn't let you have all the fun," he laughed.

"All for one, one for all," the brothers laughed, imitating the three musketeers.

"How are you here so fast and quietly?" Cathy asked Franziska.

"You have witch flight, and we have vampire speed," she smile.

The seven of them watched as the sun rose high into the sky. Albers and the others joined them.

"How is everyone feeling?" Albers asked them, looking awfully worried.

"Incredible," laughed Fillipe. "Izaak and Mikael get the football; I feel the need to run about and feel free."

"Papa, can we play football, please?" Mikael asked, he looked lost for words.

"I have one for you," Albers produced a football from behind his back.

Cathy stood with her Grandma and Franziska and watched the very handsome vampires and two young ones, running about and playing football. A natural event for most fathers, a spectacular event for vampires playing outside in the winter sunshine.

"*Mission accomplished,*" she hoped to herself.

Fillipe walked over to Cathy and took her hand. "I have no idea how we can thank you Cathy," he told her. "We will be forever in your debt. If you let us have today to get used to the outdoors, we will be at the mill in the morning to repair the portal.”

“That sounds an excellent plan. I am exhausted but running on adrenalin. I will get a lift back to my apartment and catch up on some well needed sleep.” Cathy yawned as she realised, she had been up over twenty-four hours.

“Then Miss Cathy, I will get back to the football. Tomorrow at the mill. Shall we meet at say, 10.00am. Thank you once more,” Fillipe bowed and kissed her hand.

“*I guess vampires don’t sweat either*,” Cathy thought to herself, as she watched him run back to the game of football. “*All that running around and no sweat.*”

Harold walked over to Cathy and put his arm on her arm. “Shall we take you home now?”

“Please, I am shattered. It is hard work creating all this magic.” She smiled.

The group of witches, wizards and vampires bid their farewells and left the vampires to enjoy the winter sunshine for the first time, and for some the first time in an exceptionally long time, since they were turned into vampires.

Chapter 15

Vampires Work Magic

Cathy awoke in her apartment at the mill. Oskar was still sleeping on the end of the bed.

"Wakey, wakey, sleepy," she gently nudged her cat/familiar.

"Good morning, Cathy," Oskar stretched to his full length on the bed. "you have had a good sleep; you were shattered when you got back from your successful trip to the vampires."

"What time is it?" Cathy asked, "Where is my phone?"

"It is on charge, in the kitchen, we agreed to let you sleep. The congratulations messages kept your phone beeping, so it was left in the kitchen, so it wouldn't disturb you." Oskar informed her. "It is 8.30am. You have slept straight through. You have plenty of time before your date."

"My date?" Cathy was confused. "Oh, my Grandma is in trouble now for telling tales again."

"Darling, Granddaughter." Sally appeared in the bedroom. "Did I hear my name?"

"Grandma, what have you been telling Oskar about me and Fillipe?" Cathy asked her.

"Oh Cathy, it is just a bit of harmless fun. He is incredibly handsome," Sally giggled. "Anyway, you are meeting him at 10.00am, so get yourself something special to wear."

"Grandma, stop the teasing. I am not ready for a new romance, well not yet. But I do agree with you, they are all incredibly charming." Cathy giggled.

"You have done well, releasing the vampires into the sunshine. Our ancestors have tried for so long. I knew you were special." Sally smiled. "There is a huge amount of excitement caused by the fact that the vampires are visiting the mill today."

"Shall we get ready and then go to the café? You can have some breakfast while you wait your visitors." Oskar said.

"That is the best plan you have had all day Oskar. I will shower and get dressed, then we can go and await our guests. Check out all the excitement in the place." Cathy laughed as she went to shower.

Sally and Oskar nodded to each other, they had a little plan for Adam and Tamara to be in the café, when Fillipe and his brothers arrived. A little bit of jealousy for Adam, for him to see Cathy with someone else, might just give him the reality check he needed.

Cathy did think about looking decent for the day. So instead of her denim jeans and jumper, she chose a good pair of dark trousers and a light-coloured blouse. Along with Sally and Oskar, Clara Jane, Gillian, and Harold joined them for the walk along the corridors to the café.

On reaching the café, Cathy thought it looked unusually busy for this time in the morning, But she then realised, it wasn't a normal day, it was the day the Vampire Brothers came to the mill to fix the portal – in broad daylight, all thanks to Cathy's magic.

Harold sat them all at a table near the door, rather than at Cathy's semi hidden usual table.

"Usual Cathy?" Becki came over to take the orders, of those that were eating.

Cathy's stomach did a somersault when Adam walked in with Tamara and Barney. He nodded and she replied in the same way. They took a table further inside the café, but Cathy could feel Adam's eyes watching her. More people came into the café, and Cathy realised they had come to see the vampires. A lot of people had never seen the local vampire family.

Precisely on time at 10.00am, with windows blacked out, a limousine drove into the yard.

"That must be them," Cathy said to Harold and the others that had joined them.

"Shall we go and invite then in here?" Harold stood up and beckoned Cathy to follow him.

"I guess so. I think they can drink black coffee." Cathy could feel Adam watching her, and she felt extremely uncomfortable. "Come on Harold, we have a job to do after all." She led Harold out of the café, at the same time, Albers was opening the limousine door.

First out was Fillipe, straight away, he made his way to Cathy.
"Good morning," he smiled. Cathy caught herself blushing.

"Good morning to you, Fillipe," she replied. "Welcome to Riverside Mill. Would you like some refreshment in our café before we begin?"

Tomasz and Dumar came and stood by them. Cathy could feel so many eyes on her, when she stood in the centre of the three tall and incredibly charming, attractive, elegant vampires. She could imagine what the younger girls would be saying, on the first look at the three brothers.

"That would be excellent, thank you Cathy. I shall admit, it is good to see the old mill in daylight, and not just in the darkness of the night. Boys, here now!" Dumar laughed as he shouted the two boys. "I apologise, but there was no way they were staying home today."

"Mikael and Izaak, come along and see if you would like some ice cream," Cathy told them.

"Are we allowed Papa?" Mikael asked. He was looking at the enchanted mill, thus was his first time away from the mansion. He was mesmerized.

"Of course, boys, come along." Dumar held out his hands for the boys, while Fillipe held out his hand for Cathy to take hold of. Walking back inside the café, Cathy saw everyone had turned to watch the doorway and to see the vampires close up. She also saw Adam looking directly at Fillipe and how he was holding Cathy's hand.

She kept hold of Fillipe's hand and smiled directly at Adam. *"A little bit of your own behaviour straight back at you,"* she thought to herself, and smiled.

The brothers had created a stir amongst the café's occupants, but Harold was quick to get everyone calm once more. Everyone enjoyed their drinks and chats, lots of talk about the portal and past problems. Eventually it was time to go and do the job, of fixing the portal.

"Albers, could you get the toolbox from the car please?" Fillipe asked him.

"Of course, Sir," Albers took his leave to go to the car. The mixed group of vampires, ghosts, witches, and wizards made their way out of the café, and to the entrance of the mill itself.

"Where are the boys?" Tomasz asked Dumar.

"They are in the play area, with another small boy," Dumar replied.

Cathy looked over and saw that Mikael and Izaak were laughing and playing with Barney. Her eyes caught Adam's eyes, and she thought they looked very grim. *"He should have made more of an effort to keep me, instead of falling under Tamara's lies,"* Cathy thought.

A sharp whistle from Dumar brought Cathy to her senses and the two young vampires to their father's side. "Boys, you now have to be on your absolute best behaviour. We are going into the mill and to the cellar, to the portal." Dumar explained to them. "Do you want to be part of the team or to stay here?"

"Please Papa, can we come with you. We have made a new friend; he is called Barney. Would we be able to call back in here when the portal is fixed?" Izaak asked, looking up at his father with his huge dark eyes.

"If we succeed in fixing the portal, we shall return for a celebration coffee, shall we go now?" Dumar smiled at his two sons.

Everyone made their way into the mill and through the maze of corridors. Some of the units now had the shutters open and people were busy working. *"How it is coming to life, now it is nearly Santa Season."* Cathy thought.

Fillipe was by Cathy's side at all times, she liked his protectiveness, but didn't feel ready to date again, let alone a vampire.

Cathy placed her hand on the cellar door handle, and it opened slowly to allow everyone entry to the cellar steps. Ulysses was at the bottom of the steps awaiting their arrival.

"Miss Cathy," he bowed. "Miss Sally and Clara Jane are awaiting you at the entrance to the portal. Good day to you Monsieur's Fillipe, Tomasz and Dumar. Please follow me."

Ulysess led the way to the portal door. Cathy was surprised to see not just Sally and Clara Jane waiting, but most of the members of the old coven too."

"I am sorry," Sally apologised, "but the portal has been a huge part of all our lives, and the vampires." Sally winked at Cathy.

Cathy spluttered, "Gran, you are incorrigible. Not everyone can go inside the port room today, so get the chairs out again. Then you can wait to see if it can be fixed."

"You go ahead dear," Sally smiled, "We will watch from a distance."

"Gran, you will be alongside me, if it is fixe, I will need your help with the magic." Cathy laughed.

Ulysess opened the portal door, by tapping in the code into the keypad. He led them up the ramp towards the portal.

"It has been a few decades since we were last in here," Dumar commented. "Sally, when was it you broke the portal?"

"I didn't break it," Sally gasped, "It broke itself, just like it has done now for Cathy."

"I think the portal has a minor blip, every time we have a new leader of the coven," Fillipe told them. "It is as thought the portal needs to be reprogramed for the latest ancestor in your family."

"That could be it!" Sally exclaimed, whilst smiling at Fillipe. "*Flirt,*" Cathy thought.

"Maybe that is the case, let's have a closer look what the real problem can be," Dumar laughed at Sally's response. "Boys, can you carry the toolbox between you both?"

Cathy hadn't noticed the huge metal toolbox before, she had seen Albers going to the car, but not seen anyone carry it to the cellar. "*Magic?*" she thought.

Ulysess had his guards step back from the portal, to allow the vampires to get to work.

Cathy, Sally, and Harold stood with the guards and watched the vampires do their work. Cathy and Sally watched in earnest as the vampires started to remove their jackets and rolled their sleeves up."

"Watch how they work," Sally whispered to Cathy.

"Why?" Cathy replied.

"You will soon see," Sally teased.

Cathy watched on in awe. Now she understood what Franziska meant by vampire speed. Before her eyes, the three vampires flitted from one place to the next. Faster than the eye could see. The two small vampire boys stood as still as statues, watching their elders work.

"One day, this will be those two fixing the portal, grown up and heartbreakers too." She smiled to herself.

The three older vampires flitted back and forth. All around the portal. With vampires not being able to sweat, Cathy thought the three brothers looked so cool. She could feel her own palms sweaty with anticipation.

Everyone stood and watched the brothers working, the guards were transfixed on the work being done. The portals purple mass was swirling around, busier, and faster than previously.

"I think we have solved the problem," Fillipe eventually told them.

"What was it?" Cathy enquired.

"Same as before." Fillipe told her. "It just needed a bit of a reprogramme. The last time we updated the portal, we introduced a new computer programme to the old system. It just needed an update, basically to add Cathy to the ancestor pathway. It will need a few days to settle down and then I am sure you will be able to go and visit the North Pole and get the mad Santa Season underway."

The three vampires stood back and put on their jackets. Cathy looked on, *"if only they were not vampires,"* she thought wistfully.

"Well, I sure need another drink after all that work," Dumar laughed. "Boys, how about we return to the café and have that celebration drink." He picked them both up and hugged them both.

"Oh, to be loved like that," Cathy watched them.

Sally saw the wistful look in Cathy's face, "Come along, shall we go and tell the other, who are waiting outside, and then adjourn to the café? In a couple of days, you won't know what has hit you."

Cathy said her farewells to Ulysess and his cousins and followed the group back through the mill.

Fillipe held back to wait for her. "You don't have to be alone, Cathy," he said tenderly, "But I do understand."

Blushing, Cathy smiled at him, "Shall we go and join the others, Thank you for helping me out with the portal."

"Catherine," his voice was serious, "You are the one to be thanked, not me. Look at me, I am outside, in daylight, and it is all thanks to you."

Fillipe leaned in and place a kiss on her cheek, "I am always here for you." He held her hand as they walked back to join the others in the café.

Out of the corner of her eye, she felt Adam looking at her. *"Do I still love him?"* she asked herself. *"I honestly do not know."*

Adam smiled at her, but Cathy saw Tamara take hold of his hand and lean in to give him a kiss. Probably showing Cathy, that he was hers now.

"If that is the way he wants it to be, so be it." Cathy thought.

She was soon brought back out of her thoughts, by Becki placing a hazelnut latte and piece of her favourite cake in front of her.

"Have a drink Cathy," Fillipe had been watching her, "It is time to celebrate, please ignore what that woman is trying to do to you."

"I know, deep breaths and move on." Cathy smiled at Fillipe, "I best announce that the Santa Season will be under way soon."

Cathy smiled and then made the announcement to the delight of the occupants of the café. When the applause had settled down, she saw that Adam had left the café, but Tamara and Barney where still there.

Tamara met Cathy's eyes, *"She still doesn't know who I am!"* Cathy thought. *"Well, that's a bonus."*

"She will have a shock when she finds out you are the woman that Adam loves so much" Fillipe whispered.

"Do you think that is true?" Cathy looked at the vampire.

"I am certain my dear, sadly." Fillipe smiled. "Now time to celebrate the sunshine and the portal."

Chapter 16

Tamara's exposed

The mill settled back into its usual activities. Two days after the portal problems being solved, Cathy received a text message from Brian, asking her to go and meet her at CJs Café. *"I wonder what this means?"* Cathy thought to herself when she left the apartment. She made her way through the extensive stretch of corridors, that led to the café from her apartment. Lots of the units had their shutters open and everyone spoke to Cathy as she passed by. Santa season was definitely in full flow.

Brian and Stephen were waiting for her, at her usual table, just tucked away behind the counter.

"Hi Cathy," Stephen gave her a hug, as she greeted them.

"How are you keeping?" Brian asked her.

"I am ok, keeping busy with coven duties, portals and vampires." Cathy smiled. These two men held a special place in her heart and they had worked around the clock with the magical and normal police to help uncover Tamara's family.

"The reason I messaged you to meet here, and so quickly, well, I have some news for you." Brian told her.

"Oh, what sort of news?" Cathy questioned.

"Good news. Melanie and Bob Walker were on the cruise liner that docked in Liverpool last night. When they disembarked, the normal police met them. It turns out that the cruise was paid for by her sister. Mrs Walker has a serious illness, and Tamara paid for her to go and try to relax. The couple had no idea that Tamara had plans of her own. They told the police that Tamara's second husband, Bill McIlroy passed away six months ago. There were complications with his estate. His sons from a previous marriage inherited the majority of the will. Tamara got a decent pay out, for the short time she was married to Bill. She wasn't happy, she had expected to receive everything. Anyway, they are on their way here to collect Barney." Brian brought her up to date on all the information they had learnt.

"My word, that is good news and good work. We always knew he wasn't hers." Cathy laughed as her stomach did somersaults. She hadn't spoken or seen Adam since the evening after the portal opening and vampire visit.

"When are they coming, are they coming here?" Cathy asked.

"They will be here, in the café in approximately thirty minutes. I messaged Adam to tell him to bring Tamara and Barney here for a coffee. So, it should make an interesting afternoon." Laughed Brian. "I cannot wait to see the back of that woman – again."

From their semi hidden table, Cathy saw Adam leading Barney and Tamara into the café. "*Happy family*" she thought as she saw them. He sat them in a window seat and looked around for his father. He walked over to the counter to order the drinks and saw the three of them sat at their table.

Cathy's heart did a flip when she saw Adam looking her way. She had wanted this day to happen for so long. Yet now it was here, did she still feel the same way about Adam. "*Time will tell.*" She thought, as she returned his smile. Sipping on her latte, Cathy spied Sally and Clara Jane trying to hide in the kitchen area. They sent her a thumbs up message and pointed to the café entrance.

Sergeant Dobson, from the normal police, opened the door to let a young couple through. Cathy's heart sank to see the woman, who must be Melanie, curled up in a wheelchair. "*Gosh, she looks poorly.*" Cathy thought to herself.

Just as the door closed, and Bob Walker pushed the wheelchair into the café, a small cry escaped from Barney. He flew across the café before Tamara could stop him.

"Mummy, Daddy. You are back." The small boy cried. "I have tried to be so good for Auntie Tam. I tried to play the game, but I have missed you so much."

The trio hugged and cried at this very public reunion. Tamara tried to sidle out of the seating booth she was in, but Adam stopped her. "Care to explain?" he asked her.

But, her brother-in-law, had also stood in front of her. "Tamara, what game have you been playing now?" he growled.

She stood looking at the floor, as she felt all the eyes of everyone in the café, looking at her.

"Barney, what game has Auntie Tam made you play, while we have been on the cruise?" he asked Barney gently.

"When you went away, to help Mummy get better, Auntie Tam told me we were going to play a game on Uncle Adam. She said she was going to pretend to be my mummy, and that Uncle Adam was my daddy. Uncle Adam is really nice, but Auntie Tam scares me. But Miss Cathy and Clara Jane are the best." Barney couldn't stop talking, now he was back with his mummy and daddy.

Cathy and Brian looked at each other, "Did he just say Clara Jane?" Cathy whispered.

"Yes, how can he see her?" Brian replied.

"Magic, I guess." Cathy smiled, looking over at Clara Jane who was watching her small friend Barney.

"So, Tamara, you paid for the cruise for your sister and me, so you could play yet another nasty trick on Adam?" Bob wasn't going to hold back, his disgust at his sister-in-law. "Don't you ever learn. Your last husband married you because you tricked him. How much older than you was he? Poor bugger is dead now, but you didn't succeed in getting him to change his will, did you? You got a payout, and his sons got the business and the property. But you used a small child to get back at Adam, why?"

Tamara pouted, and tried to talk, but Bob wouldn't let her. He was so angry. "How do you think we felt, when we embarked this morning, to be whisked away by the police. Do you ever think of your poor sister and how ill she is?"

"I do think of Mel, that's why I paid for the cruise for you both," Tamara cried,

"That Bill paid for, not you. You have never earned any money yourself. You ripped off Adam and then old Bill." Bob continued. "You have never had a job like normal people."

"Daddy, Mummy isn't well, she is trying to talk, but the words won't come out," a worried Barney cried, as he held on tight to his mummy.

Sergeant Dobson took out his handcuffs, "Do you want me to arrest her for impersonating and kidnapping?" he asked them.

"Not just yet, Tamara, sit at the table with Sergeant Dobson for now, we need to help Melanie." Adam told her.

"Becki," he shouted, "Can you find Cathy for me, tell her it is an emergency please."

Cathy stood up and made her way around the counter to Adam. "I am here Adam, what can I do to help?"

"Ah, the rich bitch makes an appearance at last," Tamara snarled.

"Be quiet!" Adam shouted at Tamara.

"Cathy, can you help Bob take Melanie over to the boardroom please. Barney knows you, so he can go with you too. I need to sort this out here first," Adam's voice was full of worry.

"This way please," Cathy led them out of the café and across the yard to the main reception and the boardroom. Followed closely by Sally and Clara Jane.

Harold met them at reception, and they wheeled Melanie into the adjoining boardroom.

Cathy knelt before Melanie, taking her hands in her own. Sending a drop of magic into Melanie, to help her relax. Cathy asked Bob, what her symptoms were.

Bob answered, very quietly. "Where do I start. Melanie was an active person. She had her pregnancy with Barney, with no problems, not even in labour. We were a happy family and even talking about having a sibling for Barney. I used to work with Peter and Susie the archaeologists. But when Mel started being ill, I have had to stay home to look after her and Barney. I am a full-time carer now. Her first symptoms were weak knees. She kept falling down, for no reason at all. The first doctor told her to do more exercise to strengthen the muscles. Then she lost her smile. We thought she was just unhappy, but when we tried to make her laugh and smile, she couldn't. Then her arms were like lead weights. They were so heavy; she couldn't lift them to use the hairdryer. This then lead to not swallowing food or liquids. That doctor just thought she was an alcoholic as her words slurred. How was that possible if she couldn't even drink properly. I now have to dress her and do most things for her. Look how her eyes droop, she is just like a rag doll."

Cathy's ears pricked up, "Has the doctor tested her for MS, multiple sclerosis?"

"No, sadly that is our next step." Bob sighed,

"I don't suppose they have tested for Myasthenia Gravis either?" Cathy asked.

"I have never even heard of that," Bob replied.

"My friend kate, who I lived with at Sheffield University, had all the same symptoms. It took three years, nine doctors and fifteen specialists to confirm myasthenia gravis."

"Look," Barney shouted, "Uncle Adam is here with the doctor."

"Hi Dr Tom," Cathy greeted the local doctor. "I know I am not a doctor, and I don't want to presume I can do your job. But Melanie's symptoms are remarkably similar to those of my friend Kate."

"You would make an excellent doctor Catherine," Dr Tom patted her on her shoulder. "Now let me see the patient."

Barney was prised off his mother, with a little help from Clara Jane, who took his hand and led him to a nearby chair.

Dr Tom, went to examine Mel, asking all the questions. After what felt like forever, he stood up and cleared his throat. "Cathy, I think you may be correct. We will have to take Melanie into hospital to run few checks. But if all is in order, she could have a thymectomy, which is what Kate had."

"That is brilliant," Cathy smiled and accidently hugged Adam.

"Don't stop," he whispered, but she backed away.

"Bob, you, and Barney stay with me, until Mel gets sorted at the hospital. Afterwards if you like, until she is on her feet again." Adam offered.

"Cathy, what is your friend Kate like nowadays?" Bob asked her.

"Oh, Kate, she is a total nutter, two children and happily living just a few miles away. I can introduce you if you like, then you can ask her all the questions, about life with Myasthenia Gravis." Cathy told him.

Dr Tom said to Melanie, "I want you to take two of these tablets. If they work, then we have the correct diagnosis."

Fetching a glass of water from the kitchen, Cathy helped Mel swallow the tablets. (Yes, she did use a touch of magic to help.)

"What will happen to Auntie Tam," asked Barney.

"Technically, she hadn't really broken the law. Your mum and dad gave her permission to look after you, so there was no kidnapping." "

"Perhaps, we could send her on a three-month cruise," everyone turned to see Melanie sat up in her chair and a small smile on her face.

"What was in those tablets, Dr Tom?" she asked.

"Magic," he replied with a smile. "I think we should get you to hospital and get the tests carried out. My friend is the expert in this disease. It stops your nerve endings touching the muscles. Now the medicine is called Mestion. I am hoping Cathy's diagnosis is correct."

"I think a three-month cruise for Tamara is an excellent idea," laughed Cathy. "I think the trust fund would cover the cost. Let her find herself another unsuspecting partner and keep her away from Green Valley."

Dr Tom, Mel, and Bob left for the hospital, leaving Barney with Adam, Cathy, and the others.

"Come to mine when you finish at the hospital. Tamara is with Sergeant Dobson at the police station. He is keeping her in the cell for a couple of nights, just as a small lesson." Adam said.

When everyone had left, Barney, held onto Cathy's hand. "Cathy can Clara Jane come with us too, to Uncle Adams house," his small voice asked.

"How long have you seen Clara Jane?" Cathy asked him.

"When we first arrived at Uncle Adam's house, and I had to play that game. She was in the house, with that lady stood over there." He pointed to Sally.

"Oh right," Cathy smiled, "When your Daddy gets back, we will ask him about Clara Jane. For now, you will stay with Adam, and enjoy being Barney. Your mum is in safe hands with Dr Tom."

Everyone made their way out of the boardroom. Cathy was left with her Grandma Sally.

"How are you coping?" Sally asked her.

"To be honest, Grandma. I just don't know how I feel anymore. We always knew Tamara was lying. But I just kept seeing them or imagining them together in that house. The trip to the vampires has made me doubt myself."

"Yes, the vampires have a certain effect on us witches. But I still think Adam is the one for you, just give it some time. Enjoy the vampires flirting, but remember, they are actually incredibly old men." Sally laughed as she said the last part.

"Oh, Gran, how to spoil a girl's dream. Shall we go back to the apartment, I need to double check the crystals and spell for the vampire chip. I think our job is done here." Cathy sighed and began the lonely walk back to her own apartment.

Chapter 17

Return to the Town Hall

After the events of the last couple of days, Cathy took the morning to recharge in her Temple Room. She felt like she hadn't spent enough time in here of late. She planned to meditate and recharge her crystals and her own battery,

Her phone buzzed, and it stirred her from her thoughts. *"Who is phoning me today*?" she thought. Looking at the screen, she saw it was Brownen, from the Nether Valley Coven.

"Hi Cathy," Bronwen announced down the phone. "You have remembered you are visiting us today?"

"Oh, I am so sorry. I have been so busy with the vampires, portals, and ex-wives. I had completely forgotten, "Cathy apologised.

"Do you want to cancel?" Bronwen asked her. Cathy could hear the disappointment in her voice.

"No, of course not. It is fine, give me an hour or so and I will consult my grimoire. I will use witch flight to your place, to save time on travelling." Cathy told her.

"Why not go straight to the courtroom, say around 2.00pm. I haven't told any of the others this time," Bronwen confided.

"I will ask my grandma to come with us, she has a certain way with stubborn male ghosts," Cathy giggled. "OK, 2.00pm in the courtroom."

"See you there," and Bronwen ended the call.

Sally appeared before Cathy and smiled at her granddaughter. "Life doesn't stay quiet for long, for the leaders of this coven."

"I am realising that Gran," Cathy smiled.

"We can help Bronwen and her ancestors today. Tomorrow you can step through the portal. I do wish I could go with you." Sally sighed.

"Can you not go through the portal in ghost form?" Cathy asked.

"No, I don't think it will be possible," Sally replied.

"Never say never, Gran. Maybe one day, when I know more about what my powers can do." Cathy laughed. "Anyway, we need to be at the courtroom for 2.00pm. I better ask Peter if he can make it with us, always one for some history."

Cathy made a quick phone call to the archaeologist couple, but unfortunately, they were away on a dig down in the south of the country.

Cathy gathered together her ghost whisperer bag of tricks, and started to check everything was in that she might need. Alongside her grandma, Cathy replaced a few crystals and the candles. While they concentrated on the supplies, Cathy noticed her grimoire had opened and was sparkling. Cathy went over and took the grimoire, and settled in her favourite chair, next to the altar.

Closing her eyes, she listened to the grimoire, and felt it passing on the knowledge she needed to know. She felt she was being told to be cautious about the courtroom.

"Grandma, the grimoire is telling me to be cautious, what does that mean?" she asked.

"Maybe, we have a case of more than one ghost?" Sally thought aloud.

"It is telling me to make some ties, - special sorts of ties," Cathy pondered.

"I think it means ghost ties. I remember my dad getting in too deep trying to help ghosts. The ghosts you have helped so far, have all been willing or wanting to pass over."

"Oh dear, nothing like straight forward for me," Cathy moaned.

"My darling granddaughter, life will never be simple for you, but it will be more than worthwhile. In your short time being the leader of the coven, you have done incredible things. Think of Tamara as a learning curve. It will all be sorted soon," Sally reassured her granddaughter.

"Come along then Gran, show me how to make these ghost ties. Is it a bit like the bullies at the mill when we freed Clara Jane? They were banished rather than pass over?" Cathy asked.

"Look at how quick you are learning. It is exactly like that. Ask the grimoire that we actually need?" Sally smiled.

Gathering together more crystals and candles, Cathy got some twine that was on one of the benches in the Temple Room and began to make up a few sets of the specific ghost ties, as instructed by the grimoire.

At exactly 2.00pm. Cathy and Sally prepared to make their witch flight to the Nether Valley Town Hall. When she got her balance back, and opened her eyes, Cathy saw Bronwen stood in front of her, smiling at her.

"Welcome back to Nether Valley. Huge congratulations on getting the vampires outside and the portal fixed. I hope we can bring some peace to the courtroom today. Isn't Peter with you?" Bronwen asked.

"No, he and Susie are on a weeklong dig, and were gutted to miss out." Cathy updated her. Cathy smiled, she did enjoy this part of her new life, helping lost souls pass over peacefully. "I have brought my grimoire and extra supplies. The grimoire gave me a kind of warning, we have to be aware of more than just your ancestor."

Sally was floating around the room, "Girls, come over her," she motioned them to an area near the judges chair.

"This is the old staircase that the prisoners were brought from the cellars and cells." Brownen informed them.

"No wonder it feels cold here. So many bad people have walked through this place," Cathy sighed. "We must leave one of the ghost ties here, stop anything untoward."

"Good idea Cathy," Sally smiled as she knew her granddaughter would automatically know what to do.

"We need to go all around the courtroom, and see if we can find anymore cold spots, then leave a ghost tie in each place," Cathy instructed.

In all they found three more cold spots around the courtroom. One was in the witness box, one on the row of seats near the juries bench and a final one at the back of the room. The one at the back of the room, confused them all. The witness box, staircase and jury's bench made some sense, as that was where the prisoners would have been near.

"We will find out when we start the passing over ceremony," Cathy told the others.

"Now that the ghost ties are all in place, that should hold off anything unexpected. Shall we now commence and stand near the judge's chair. As she moved back to the front of the courtroom, Cathy sprinkled a drop of water while she walked.

"What is in the water?" Bronwen asked, curious of all that Cathy did.

"I have mixed the water with some essential oils. Lavender, Frankincense, and a few others." Cathy explained. "I want to create a pleasant atmosphere."

When they arrived at the judges chair, Cathy chalked a large pentacle on the floor. A five-sided star, in a circle. The five points represent the five elements of air, fire, water, earth, and spirit, enclosed with a circle of protection.

Placing candles at each point of the star, Cathy lit them as she began to chant her spell.

Cathy, Sally and Bronwen, stood back-to-back, forming a circle, inside the pentacle. Their eyes scanning each corner of the courtroom.

"Keep an eye on the ghost ties," Sally reminded the girls. "they should do the trick, until we can deal with any untoward spirits."

"I will concentrate on the Judge," Cathy told them. Walking from the pentacle to the judges chair, Cathy asked for any ghosts to show themselves. The courtroom was silent and very still.

"Your honour, Judge Robinson, could you show yourself please. I am Cathy Collins, the ghost whisperer of Green Valley." Cathy spoke slowly and quietly; she did not want to disturb any other ghosts.

Nothing happened, just stillness. Cathy tried again, but there was just an eery silence.

Sally whispered in Cathy's ear. "This is the same presence as the bullies at the mill. I will go and fetch Betty and Dessie, for back up. That way, if necessary, we will have more magic. They helped banish the bad ones at the mill."

Before Cathy could reply, her grandma had disappeared.

"Is everything alright?" Bronwen asked, concerned at Sally's quick departure.

"We think there are other ghosts present and they are stopping your ancestor from showing himself to us. Sally has gone for two of her old friends, they banished the bad bully ghosts from the mill." Cathy explained.

Before she could finish explaining, Sally along with Dessie and Betty had arrived in the courtroom, and another bag of witchy items.

"Not to worry Cathy," Betty laughed, "you did it before, you can do it again today. We are only here to make up numbers and have an afternoon out."

The two older witches circled the room and saw the ghost ties in place.

"Perfect Cathy, you have done well," Dessie (Desdemona) acknowledged.

"Now if we make a pentacle a bit bigger, adjoining the original one, we can all stand at the star points." Betty said, as she organised the younger witches.

"Now, ask them all to appear, but ask Judge Robinson to stay hidden." Dessie continued.

Taking a deep breath, Cathy stood on the pentacle, "Show yourself, whoever you are." Cathy said aloud in a sterner voice. All niceties were gone now that she knew she was dealing with bad spirits.

"Show yourselves to the Covens of Nether Valley and Green Valley members." Cathy continued, "What is it you seek, by remaining in this room, in your after life?"

Gradually Cathy could feel the air around her grow cold. She glanced over to the old staircase to the cellar. She made out the outline of an exceptionally large man ghost.

"Who are you coming in here causing trouble?" the gruff voice shouted.

"Yea, who are you, little girl," an aggressive voice came from the witness box.

"Oh, I see you both now, bullies in death as well as in life." Cathy taunted. She knew a ghost couldn't physically harm her, and she was no longer scared of ghosts.

"Come here and introduce yourselves to me," Cathy spoke to them.

"I can't move, you have me all tied up, release me NOW, you witch," the gruff voice shouted, beginning to panic.

"Same her, I can't move from the spot," the voice in the witness box spluttered.

"Oh. Well, that is a shame," Cathy laughed, "Yes, I am a witch and immensely proud of my ancestry. But I am also a ghost whisperer, but my guess is, you don't want to pass over peacefully, you want to stay and taunt Judge Robinson. Did he sentence you both, by any chance?"

"Oh, don't you know it all, you witch," the gruff voice growled.

"Well, it doesn't take a genius to work it out. Tell me your names and your crimes?" Cathy asked.

"Find out yourself, you bloody nuisance of a witch," gruff told her.

"OK. That is what I shall do," Cathy sat on the floor in the centre of the pentacle. She got her grimoire from her bag and closed her eyes. Soon she was felling the magic surge through her arms and body. Soon three names came to mind.

"Let me see, you on the stairwell, are George Barnes, sentence to life for grievous bodily harm whilst robbing someone. You in the witness box are his brother, Bill Barnes, same sentence. But you, sat on the jurors bench, you are called Bert Jones. You were sentenced to death for the shooting of Judge Robinson. Show yourself, you coward." Cathy pointed to the jurors bench.

The vaporization of Bert Jones slowly turned into the ghost of a man. "How the hell do you know all that?" Bert confronted her, "You are a witch!"

"We have already established, that I and my colleagues are all witches, have you not been listening to the conversation? I am from a long ancestry of witches, with powers to banish the three of you, to a place where you will soon wish you had never gone to." Cathy told the ghost of Bill Jones.

"You cannot do that, you're just a silly young kid," Bert argued.

"Oh, please don't test her patience," Sally couldn't help laughing.

"Oh, my word, you are a ghost," Bert cowered.

Sally laughed again, "A ghost cowering from another ghost. Bless you Bert, Cathy, do your magic."

"Wait," George Barnes started.

"Say your goodbyes boys," Dessie language, "Where you're going, you won't have anyone to bully every again, you will be all alone."

"Wait," Geroge Barnes started again.

"Nothing to wait for. This young witch has had enough of your rudeness, now be off with all of you." Cathy told him, whilst she was lighting a set of coloured candles. She lit each candle and started the banishment chant. Bronwen and the others joined in. As the chanting got lounder, the air turned dark and black tendrils of smoke reached out and held onto the three ghosts. The ghost ties gripped tighter as they squeezed tight.

Cathy watched as they disappeared into who knew where.

"Is that what happened at the mill?" she asked the elders.

"Pretty much the same. Not a nice sight, but it is a perfect ending to the ghosts it does happen to," Dessi told her.

"What happens, if the ghost isn't really bad?" Cathy was concerned she might send someone by mistake.

"The banishment spell won't work on anyone that is good. They would still be here after the spell completes," Dessie put Cathy's worries to rest.

Bronwen let out a gasp, while the others were collecting the ghost ties and crystals.

"Cathy," she gasped, while pointing to the front of the room.

"Good afternoon, Miss Catherine," a jolly sturdy man had appeared before them.

"Good afternoon your honour," Cathy replied.

"Thank you for clearing the air with those three troublesome men. Where have you sent them?" the judge asked,

"They have been banished, they will now spend eternity in a dark place, alone." Sally chipped in.

"You are also a ghost," the judge asked Sally.

"Yes, I am, and Cathy is my granddaughter, just like Bronwen is your ancestor. Can I ask, why are there four cold spots, but only three bullies?" Sally replied.

"Well, a long story about the bullies. Bert Jones was the one who pulled the trigger, a cowardly man. George Barnes was the instigator. He was the Mr Big and didn't like getting caught. He and his brother were sentenced to ten years. He then set up Bert Jones to shoot me, on his behalf."

"But what or who is at the back of the room?" Cathy asked, collecting the last of the ghost ties.

"That my dear, is my beloved wife, Brodie. She was in court the day I was shot, and the occasion more or less killed her, she died a few weeks after of a broken heart. She has been hiding at the back of the room ever since, waiting for the day we can both be reunited." Judge Robinson smiled. "Cathy, do you think it is possible you could bring her to me?"

"Now the others have gone, and the ghost ties removed, We can but try." Cathy reassured him. "Bronwen, come with me, shall we go and free your Great Grandmother Brodie?"

The group of witches walked to the back of the courtroom, with Judge Robinson floating alongside of Sally. "Oh, to be free again," he chortled.

A smaller pentacle was drawn, and Cathy began to chant, slowly but surely a figure gradually became clearer in front of them all.

"About bloody time," a small fragile looking woman began.

"Brodie, my love, I have missed you so much." Judge Robinson was beside his wife, within seconds. "Cathy has banished the three rough lads; we are together at last."

"Cathy," the Judge asked, "Can we stay around a bit longer, like Sally. I would love to get to know Bronwen."

"Actually, that is a fine idea," Cathy laughed. "I have a friend who would love to meet you but couldn't be here today. I think our job is done here, Bronwen, I will leave you with your ancestors. I will return in a short time and bring Peter to have a chat. Any problems, just call."

"Thank you, Cathy," Bronwen hugged her.

"Thank you, Cathy," The judge and his wife repeated too.

"Mission accomplished," Bronwen laughed. "you get back to the mill and rest, you have the portal trip tomorrow. So exciting. I am looking forward to spending time with the Judge and Brodie!"

Chapter 18

Through the Portal

After reuniting Bronwen with her ancestors, Cathy did a witch flight back to the mill, and then headed for the café. Using magic made her hungry. She sat at her usual seat; half hidden from the rest of the café. She saw Adam with Barney and his dad, and wanted to ask how Melanie was doing, but didn't feel she had the courage to speak to Adam, not just yet.

After eating, she sneaked out of the café, via the kitchen door that lead into the corridor. She wandered back to her apartment. A long soak, and some meditation is she wanted tonight. Her nights had become quite lonely since she split with Adam.

Eventually, morning sun rose, and the day arrived for her to go through the portal. With Sally not being able to go through in ghost form, Cathy had asked her Uncle John to go with her. He was delighted to accompany her.

The pair found themselves in front of the now swirling purple working portal. "*I do hope it works,*" Cathy thought.

"It will," her grandma's voice reassured her. "Relax and enjoy. Say hello to everyone for me."

"Gran, get out of my head," Carthy smiled. "Well, Uncle John, I suppose we had better make our move."

Cathy smiled as she held his hand.

"Thank you for this unique opportunity," he told her.

"Thank you for looking after me for all these years." Cathy replied.

Taking a look around at all her friends, that were sat in the portal room, waiting for Cathy to go through. "Here goes," she told them.

"Just step through," Sally spoke aloud rather than by using telepathy this time." It is quite simple."

Taking a giant leap into the unknown Cathy and John stepped forward. Looking at each other, they simultaneously stepped forward. Not losing a grip on each other's hands, they stepped into the purple swirling mass. Neither of them had stepped through a portal before.

The purple mist enveloped them both. *"Keep moving,"* Cathy thought to herself.

One step, two step and three steps and …

"Oh, my word," Cathy gasped, as they came out of the other side of the portal. Snow covered the ground. The sky was so clear and beautiful, but it was dark like nighttime. Red, yellow, green and purples swirls of light flew across the sky.

"Is that the northern lights?" Cathy gasped, as did her Uncle. "We have made it. But what now?"

She need not have worried, not long after stepping through the portal, a small group of people made their way over to greet them.

They were led by a portly old man, with a huge white beard.

"Cathy, you have made it at last. Welcome to the North Pole. Ho, Ho, Ho," he laughed.

Cathy relaxed; she knew right away who this man was. "Thank you," she said. "This is my Uncle John, but Grandma Sally told me to tell you she ends her love to you all."

"Sally, my hero, how we loved that woman." Santa laughed at his memories. "We have brought a couple of sleighs to take us back to our home and the workshop."

Santa whistled and two reindeers came forward pulling two sleighs.

"Dancer, take Miss Cathy and her Uncle. Guys, put these rugs over your knees, it gets a bit nippy. I will let Prancer take me and the missus back. The others can follow," guffawed Santa.

"You really have reindeers and with those names?" Cathy asked, still in awe of her surroundings.

"Oh yes, they are spoilt throughout the year, and trained especially for the Christmas Eve run. I will introduce you to the others later." Santa laughed.

"Wow, I get to meet the Santa and his reindeers," thought Cathy.

The sleigh sled through the snowy landscape, and the Northern Lights danced across the horizon.

"Uncle John. Can you pinch me, I feel like I am dreaming." Cathy laughed. "Here we are on a sleigh, pulled by Dancer, following Santa and his wife."

After a short sleigh ride, they stopped, and Santa helped Cathy and John out of the sleigh. In front of them was a shorter lady, with a long red cape.

"Welcome to our house, Miss Cathy. Call me Eva, the word knows me as Mrs Claus, Mother Christmas among other things. But amongst friends, I am Eva, and of course he is just Nick. Good old Nick." Eva laughed as she saw Cathy was still in awe.

"Thank you for having us," Cathy muttered.

"Don't worry, it takes a while for it all to sink in, that this is all real." Eva told her. "But we thank you for coming to visit. You and your family and ancestors are like our family. You have helped us so much over the years. Your ancestor was the one that created the first portal. Now we have many all around the world. I cannot tell you how much easier that has made the organisation of Christmas presents, so much easier. Even the elves are happier, now that all the toys and presents are ready made and labelled."

"I have never thought of it like that before," Cathy admitted, while she followed Eva / Mrs Claus into her house. The house was a lot bigger on the inside, than it looked from the outside.

The entrance hall was just like Cathy would imagine for Santa. Huge, with wood panelling. The smell of cinnamon, hit Cathy's nose.

"Before we start the tour, shall we have a hot chocolate, with a cinnamon bun, or two?" Eva laughed.

Cathy noticed her uncle John and Nick/Santa laughing like old friends. Eva led them into a huge kitchen, complete with a kitchen island in the centre.

Pouring cups of hot chocolate into mugs, and then producing a plate of cinnamon buns, Eva loved welcoming new guests. Slowly Cathy relaxed and smiled as she looked around the kitchen island, she was sat with Santa and his lovely wife. It seemed the most natural thing for her to be doing. When she tasted the cinnamon bun, Cathy felt it melt in her mouth.

"MMM, oh these are amazing," she mumbled, with a mouth full of soft sticky dough.

"I made them especially my dear, they were always a favourite of Sallys. I have a box of them for you to take back with you. I know, as a ghost she cannot eat them, but you can describe them to her." Eva winked as she thought of her old friend. But she could already see in Cathy, she was as good, if not even better that Sally. The power she felt of this young witch was immense.

Eventually, after lots of talk of Riverside Mill and its occupants, Santa began the tour of his workshop and the reindeer stables.

When they reached the reindeer stables, Cathy laughed as she saw the names over each stable.

"Dasher, Dancer, Comet, Vixen, Prancer, Cupid, Donner, Blitzen, and at the end of the stable block was Rudolph's stable.

"Yes, a drum roll for the most famous reindeer of all," Santa laughed.

A small reindeer strode to the front of the stable, "Good day Miss Cathy, we are all very pleased to meet you and to serve you," Rudolph spoke in a very posh English voice.

Taken aback by a talking reindeer, Cathy shook herself.

"A pleasure to meet you Rudolph and all of you," Cathy began. "I never expected that you could talk, so I am a little speechless.

"Do not be afraid, Miss Cathy. We were taught to speak by your ancestor. She thought it would help Santa with his deliveries." Rudolph laughed.

"An early form of GPS system," Blitzen told her.

"They never told us that in school," Cathy laughed with them.

"You can rest assured, we only talk out loud in the present company," Rudolph said.

"They are all an excellent help to me Cathy, especially on Christmas Eve, when we are delivering." Santa beamed, like a proud father. "To me they are all joint favourites. Just that song about Rudolph's nose and it being red. Reindeers have densely packed blood vessels near the surface of the skin, it regulates the body temperature in the extreme cold. It appears red sometimes. Sorry to spoil the legend."

"I love them all just the same too," Cathy laughed as she gave Rudolph a quick stroke over his soft dense fur.

"Right, shall we continue our tour, next to the elves and the workshop." Santa led the way from the stable block, to enter through a huge door into the workshop.

"Why is this door so big?" Cathy asked.

"This is the door that all the parcels arrive from the portals. Once deliveries start, a conveyor belt from each portal join and enter through this gateway." Santa explained.

"Oh," Cathy replied, trying to work out how big the conveyor belt would be.

Uncle John and Santa walked through the gateway, while Cathy's imagination worked overtime.

"Don't worry yourself Cathy, the conveyor belts are magic, they don't touch the ground or the snow. They appear as and when they are needed. You will return and see them in use soon." Santa reassured her.

"Oh, I will be back," Cathy told him. "I already know and feel why my grandma loved this place so much. It actually feels like magic should feel. I wish I could bottle up this feeling."

Following Santa, they went through a series of doors, and Cathy found herself in 'Santa's Workshop.' At the last set of doors, Santa handed her a pair of ear defenders.

"Put these on, if can get noisy in here," he told her.

Cathy realised the need for the ear defenders when she stepped into the workshop. In front of her were rows and rows of workers. Elves. But not dressing in red and white strips. Normal clothes, but smaller in size.

Row after row of workbenches, hammering, stretching, mending, soldering, banging!

"Santa," asked Cathy, "if you have all the portals from all around the world, what are the elves making?"

"The portals bring in the presents for the children of the world, that have asked for them. The elves make the presents for the poor, orphaned or just children in need. Everyone is catered for, no one should be left out." Santa replied,

"That is wonderful," agreed Cathy.

They walked miles around the workshop. Stopping every now and again, to speak to the workers. The elves appeared to be very conscientious works, although appearing quite small in stature.

Eventually Santa led them back to the kitchen, where Eva was waiting for them.

"I have made you some afternoon tea, for your enjoyment before you leave us." Eva told them. "I do hope you have enjoyed your first look around the place."

"It has been incredible," Cathy smiled. "Now I know why my grandma was so enthusiastic about visiting. Thank you so much for letting us come through the portal."

"Cathy, it is you who we thank, you and your family for making all this possible." Santa told her.

"We will be able to come back again?" Cathy asked.

"Whenever you like to visit, even in the cold season, you will be more than welcome. Any time you want a short break, just pop through the portal. We have a guest lodge that you can stay over in, go sledging, watch the northern lights, relax, or even go dipping in the frozen lakes." Santa guffawed.

After an appropriate amount of time had passed, Cathy and Uncle John followed Santa and Eva back to the sleighs. Arriving back at the portal, Cathy took a final look at the Northern Lights.

"They truly are as beautiful as I imagined, she sighed. "Until next time."

"Remember Cathy, there is an open invitation to come and stay with us. The Lights will put on a show for you." Eva held her hand.

"Thank you, both of you," Cathy hugged them as they stood in front of the portal.

Cathy held her Uncle's hand, and they once more, stepped towards the portal.

When they emerged at the other side, Sally was there to greet them.

"Tell me all about it," she gushed.

"Look Gran, a box of cinnamon buns for you from Eva." Cathy grinned, whilst holding the box out to her grandma.

"That woman, she does not lose her sense of humour. I bet she told you to describe them to me too, just make sure I am near when you devour them." Sally laughed. "Now shall we go and tell the others all about your adventures?"

Sally led the way out of the portal room, to the others that had been waiting for her return, amongst them was Adam and Brian, his father.

Cathy smiled at the group of witches and wizards, awaiting to hear of her journey. Out of the corner of her eye, she saw her Uncle John go over and kiss Margaret, who had been waiting for him.

"Will I ever get love back again," she thought to herself, as she saw Adam smile at her. *"No time to feel sorry for myself, time to tell the world about the North Pole and get the Santa Season underway."*

"Ladies and Gentlemen," Cathy announced to the group, "I can confirm that Santa Season is well and truly underway."

Cheers and hugs went around the room. Adam and Cathy glanced at each other but didn't get near to each other.

Eventually she saw him leave the cellar, her heart gave a quick flip.

"Onwards and upwards girl. I may not have the log cabin next to the giants, but I have a portal to the North Pole." She smiled to herself and went round to tell everyone still there about the portal.

With her grandma by her side, Cathy recounted the story of the reindeers, the northern lights, and the workshop.

"Mission accomplished gran," she whispered to her grandma.

"Another mission accomplished Cathy," smiled Sally.

Chapter 19

Museum, Cold Spots and Canal Display

Within days of the portal being officially opened, Riverside Mill had changed totally. Gone were all the closed shutters, everywhere people were working. The large warehouse which had been closed until this time, had it's roller shutter doors wide open. Trucks and containers were arriving all the time. The staff were working on a twenty-four-hour shift pattern.

Cathy was on her way to the café, to meet the archaeologists, today was the opening of the display at the museum for the canal navvies.

Walking through the mill Cathy saw that all the people were working so hard, everyone was so happy. No moaning or feeling sorry for themselves, that they had to work. People were singing along to the radio that was blaring out, whistling as they walked around. Down in the cellar, Ulysess and his cousins were busy loading the new conveyor belt that dropped from the warehouse to the cellar.

"Where has that come from?" Cathy had asked on one of her many visits.

"It is your ancestors magic," laughed Ulysess. "Even the portal is many times the size now Miss Cathy, Follow the new ramp, that the conveyor uses to get to the portal."

Cathy had been back to the North Pole a couple of times, each time it amazed her. But now the conveyors where all up and running, and parcels from all around the world were arriving. The speed that everyone worked was fascinating too.

Cathy had followed Ulysses' instructions and had gone to the side of the portal room and saw there was a hole in the wall, that led into the portal room itself. "It looks like a metal detector at the airport security checks." She told him.

"That is exactly what it is, we have to ensure every parcel that we send is genuine." Ulysess had pointed out.

Cathy loved her trips to the cellar, but today she had to walk past the door, and head to the café. Peter and Susie were waiting for her.

"Hi Cathy, we ordered you a hazelnut latte," Susie shouted her over. Walking to the table Cathy smiled to the couple.

"Hello, how are you both, you missed a good time at the courtroom, but the Judge and his wife are hanging around for a bit, so you can go and grill him over the history of the place." Cathy laughed.

"Excellent," Peter laughed. "I heard you had a bit of fun with some other ghosts too?"

"Oh yes we did, but they won't trouble us again." Cathy told them, as she drank her coffee. "But the courtroom is a wonderful place, it needs to be turned into a museum of its own."

"Talking of museums, we had better get going." Susie mentioned. "I have the drawing and medals in the car. Let's hope you find a few more ghosts today, you said there were some cold spots at the museum."

"Can't I have a day off?" Cathy pleaded.

"No," cried both of the archaeologists.

"Thanks, and I thought you were friends." Cathy laughed. "I have brought my bag of tricks, just in case."

"Brilliant, let's get on our way, Glynis will be waiting." Susie stood to leave. Looking over at Adam, Susie shrugged at Cathy, "You still not speaking?"

"It is complicated," Cathy shrugged, "can we leave it for now please."

"But Tamara has gone now, and you didn't take up the vampire on his offer?" Susie continued.

"Susie, leave it," Peter told her. "What is meant to be, will be, give them time. We need to get to Upper Valley."

Jumping into the old tatty Land Rover, which Peter continued to drive, Susie gave Cathy a hug and apologised.

"This is the picture I made of Gabriel and Adebayo, what do you think?" Susie passed Cathy a framed drawing.

"Susie, this is incredible, you have the likeness perfect. I know people will think it is just imagination, but we know it is them. They would love this," Cathy was pleased.

Arriving at the Upper Valley Museum, Glynis and a few of her coven members were waiting for them.

"Welcome back," Glynis greeted them. "I am so excited to be part of this new display. We have prepared the perfect area for you to show off the medals."

Leading the way into the museum, via the public entrance, Cathy saw that a few local people had come to see the new display. "*I better keep the magic to a minimum*," she thought to herself.

Cathy followed the small procession into the main display room of the museum. In a corner near the floor to ceiling window, was a new display stand.

"Will this be alright for you?" Glynis asked.

"Absolutely, I have the medals in a display box and the drawing of how we think the brothers might have looked like. Also, we found a newspaper clipping of the brothers bodies being found in the canal." Susie took charge, "I have tried to put together a small history of their lives."

Leaving Susie and Peter to set up the new display, Cathy and Glynis went for a walk around the museum, leaving the locals to watch the display being set up. Peter kept them entertained with the archaeology dig that found the medals.

"Do you feel anything unusual Cathy?" Glynis asked.

"Nothing, but I would like to go to the areas we visited at Mabon." Cathy replied. "They were on a lower floor I think."

"Oh yes, near the exhibit of the eighteenth-century cottage, or maybe the Victorian living room," Glynis eagerly suggested.

"Yes, I want to start at the old weavers cottage, I love that exhibit and always feel drawn to it." Cathy replied.

The pair headed towards the small cluster of reconstructed rooms.

"Feel anything?" Glynis asked again.

"Nothing," Cathy smiled, "Maybe I get a day off."

"No chance." Glynis giggled, "I want you to find some cold spots to investigate."

"Oh, stop it, you are getting as bad as Susie and Peter. Always wanting me to be working." Cathy groaned.

When they neared the cluster of small, recreated rooms, Cathy glanced at each exhibit, and then around the exhibition hall, to check if any members of the public were in with them.

"Glynis, shall we go to the old Victorian cottage room first." Cathy whispered.

"What is it?" Glynis whispered back.

"I am not sure, but look over there in the room, there are two golden orbs bobbing about," Cathy pointed to two circles of light. "Like the old photos, you can sometime see a ball of light. It is said that it is the spirit of a loved one. A manifestation of their energy, sometimes they are called ghost orbs. At least they seem to be glowing orbs, suggesting someone is trapped and needs rescuing. Black orbs can be negative or angry spirits."

"I never knew that there were different types and colours of orbs." Glynis said, whilst she watched the two orbs bouncing around in the reconstructed old weaver's cottage.

"I think we need to investigate. I feel they are beckoning us over to them," Cathy wandered nearer the exhibit.

The exhibit was a reconstruction of a 1820s one bed cottage, basically just one room. It had a bed that could be lowered from the ceiling in the evening. A cast iron fire range that was used for cooking and the heating. Large copper bottom pans were on display, similar to the ones that would have been used. A small table, with a heavy cloth over it, with a vase and flowers.

Moving closer, Cathy felt the orbs getting bigger.

"I am scared," Glynis stuck close to Cathy. "Having only seen my grandma being a ghost, I am all new to all this."

"It is ok, they are just trapped in their orbs. Do you think we should get Peter and Susie, or let them occupy the public at the display, while we deal with this? Cathy asked her."

"I think we should do it now; they look agitated," Glynis whispered.

Glynis went to lock the door, so the public wouldn't disturb anything, whilst Cathy did her work.

Cathy laid out her candles and crystals in front of the exhibition room. Together the two young witches held hands and stood inside the pentacle, that Cathy had chalked upon the floor.

"Hello," Cathy began, "I can see your orbs, would you like to show yourselves. I am Cathy Collins the Ghost Whisperer. I can help you pass over if that is what you desire."

Cathy thought hard and summoned her own grandma. Within seconds she was there, accompanied with Glynis's ghostly grandma Sarah.

Glynis let out a huge sigh, and whispered, "Oh, am I please to see you two. I have not been with Cathy when she helps the ghosts before."

It is all right; you will be safe. Just watch and learn," Sarah told her.

Cathy continued to try to persuade the two orbs to return to their human like state. "I have helped Gabriel and Adebayo pass over, in fact we are setting up a display today downstairs, explaining a bit of the life story. Do you not think it would be good to finally leave this room and be reunited with your own family?"

Sally stepped into the entrance of the exhibit. "I remember a family being moved from the farm, when they built the golf course, they had to move out to make way for the workers. A lot of the furniture from there was used to recreate this room, back in the 1960s. When the museum first opened. This room has been here since the beginning."

"Do you think it could be possible that the two orbs, actually came with the furniture?" Sarah asked.

Cathy knew the two ghostly grandmothers were trying to coax out the occupants of the two orbs, reminiscing of the beginning of the museum.

"I am not so sure," Cathy joined in the conversation. "Why would two ghosts be stuck in some old furniture?" Cathy then noticed the orbs dancing around, trying to get her attention. She stepped out of the pentacle and joined the two ghosts in the entrance to the exhibit. "That old fireplace could tell a tale or two and look at the bed hung up in the rafters. It is so amazing to have such history that has lasted so long. The owners must have looked after it all very lovingly."

The orbs were so close to Cathy, she could almost touch them. "It is a shame that I am the ghost whisperer, and I cannot help these two. We might as well pack up and go back to the canal display,"

Cathy reluctantly began to pack up the candles and crystals. Sally whispered to her, "Not everyone wants to be helped."

The two orbs moved to the edge of the exhibit but couldn't move out of the actual room.

Sally noticed this, and motioned Cathy to look too. "Do you think they could be locked in the room, actually unable to leave the exhibit?" Sally asked.

"I never thought of that," Cathy admitted. "I just assumed they didn't want to move on. What can I do now?"

"Why not try the revealing spell, to show hidden barriers?" Sally suggested.

Replacing the crystals and candles, Cathy got a few more from her bag. Together with Glynis, they practised the spell a few times. After a few more minutes, they moved back to the opening of the exhibit room.

Saying the spell out loud together, eventually a fine white cloud appeared around the orbs. A mist covered the entrance to the old cottage. Through the mist they could see intricate lines woven around some of the furniture in the room.

"My word," exclaimed Sally. "I haven't seen that sort of black magic for an exceptionally long time. It was banned centuries ago."

"That looks like the work of Old Doris," Sarah agreed.

"What can we do and who was Old Doris?" Cathy asked the pair of ghosts.

"She was an old crone that lived like a hermit, not that far from Philips Farm. Think of the golf course and right at the far end, I do believe the old gate posts are still there for the farm. She was never satisfied with her life, and eventually gave way to using black magic. Not welcome by our ancestors she was the original wicked witch. We were taught about her when we were young, how not to be." Sally continued. "Sadly, she never forgave her family, even though she was the bad apple in the pack. It will be her keeping the orbs attached to the furniture."

"How do we set them free?" Cathy asked,

"That is simple. Our ancestors have all inherited the 'Anti Doris' spell work, more out of necessity in the early days." Sally laughed, "I am going to enjoy seeing this, I never got the chance to use it myself. Right, Cathy and Glynis in the middle, Sarah, and myself at the end of the line. Together we will just ask for the spell to be reversed,"

"If it is that simple, why hasn't it been done before?" Cathy questioned.

"Simple answer, it has been your magic that have brought out the orbs. None of us have that kind of magic." Sally explained. "Right, when we are all ready."

"Now," Cathy cried,

The four repeated the reversing spell and watched on as the tendrils of the intricate lines, sparked and fizzed.

"Look, it is working," shouted Glynis. "The lines are fizzing, and the mist is clearing.

When the mist cleared and the lines had all burnt out, in front of the witches stood two women, from a few centuries ago.

"Thank you so much, my dear," the tallest of the two middle aged ladies spoke.

"Hello," Cathy said hesitantly to the two new ghosts.

"We are Ester and Ruth; Doris was our older sister. We did live at the homestead. Doris met one of those fellas from out of town, that was working on the railroad. Irish he was. We told her he was no good, but she was bored of the simple life at home. Weaving all week and going to church on Sundays. She left with him, in the middle of the night. A few years later she returned. Ruth and I never married, and Ma and Pa never got over losing their eldest, Doris." Ester told them.

"What happened then?" Sally asked.

"You are a ghost?" Ruth asked in awe.

"Yes, Cathy is my granddaughter, and she is the ghost whisperer." Sally told her,

Ruth continued their story, "Well, she returned from her travels, a couple of years later. Needless to say, that he had turned out just as we said. Sadly, Ma and Pa both had passed away. The two of us ran the farmstead. We lived a pleasant simple life, just the two of us. Until she returned, she wanted all that we had built up on the farm. With her being the eldest, she said it was all hers. We put up a fight, but she cursed us with her black magic."

"Sorry, did you know that witches existed?" Ester asked the group.

"We are all witches, there is no need to be afraid," Cathy reassured them.

"Really, that is exciting," Ester laughed for the first time in a long time. "Well, she cursed us to a life of eternity at the cottage. Let us do all the work and running about, but when we passed on, she locked us into the furniture. We never left the house after she returned, except when they demolished the house and brought the furniture here. But because we were cursed by her, we have spent eternity with the furniture."

"When you arrived today, and could actually see our orbs, I was so excited. You are the first to see through her magic." Ruth babbled excitedly.

"Would you like to pass over and join your other relatives?" Cathy asked the sisters, "To be finally at peace?"

"Oh yes, that would be perfect." Ester smiled. "But could we stay around a few days, to look around the area and see what changes have been made. We have only looked out of this cube for the last sixty years or so."

"What do you think Glynis, the museum is your domain," Cathy laughed.

"Grandmas Sally and Sarah will show you around the place, but invisible please so you don't frighten any of the members of the public." Glynis told them.

"Marvellous," Ester clapped her tiny hands, "Ruth, we are going to live a little at long last."

The sisters hugged each other and then disappeared into the ether with Sally and Sarah. |Leaving Cathy and Glynis alone. Packing up the equipment Glynis laughed and said, "Well that was different."

"I am glad our grandmas arrived, it would have taken some working out that dark magic was at work, shall we go and get back to Susie and Peter and the new display." Cathy suggested. "We can update them after. With Ester and Ruth staying around for a while, we can introduce them later."

"It looks like Upper Valley Coven has its own ghost community now," laughed Glynis. "Just like Riverside Mills and the Nether Valley town hall."

Walking back into the main exhibition hall, they were just in time to see the unveiling of the new exhibit. Cathy was sure she heard a gasp from the back of the room. Turning she saw the two sisters looking at the drawings of Adebayo and Gabriel.

"Well, well," thought Cathy, *"I wonder if they knew each other, but that is a question for another day."*

Chapter 20

Santa Madness

The madness of Santa Season did not slow down. Each day Cathy was called upon to solve problems, give advice and visit the portal. Daily trips to the North Pole, included sampling Eva's cooking.

The days flew by and soon it would be the winter solstice, and then Christmas will arrive. Cathy could see Santa getting agitated as Christmas Eve drew nearer.

"Ignore him," Eva laughed, "He is like this every year. But since your ancestors helped with the portals. Everything runs like clockwork now."

"I would be worried too, it is an enormous task delivering all the presents," Cathy replied.

"It runs like clockwork, my dear girl," Eva smiled. "Now drink your hot chocolate whilst you have the time."

"True, I never seem to stop these days. I never realised being the Protector of the Portal was such a huge job." Cathy sipped her hot chocolate and let out a sigh.

"It will soon be over, and you have the winter solstice party to look forward to. That is the last day of the seasonal madness. It all calms down for the next couple of days, until present delivery day." Eva explained. "I do wish I could see your grandmother again; she was such a good friend."

"Maybe you can visit us after the season finishes. Come and stay in one of Harold's new log cabins, they are just being finished off." Cathy suggested. "You can go through the portal too?"

"I don't know. We have never tried," Eva pondered.

"Well, I bet if I came and took you both through, it would work," Cathy suggested.

"That is an interesting idea, wait until I tell Nick," Eva busied herself in the kitchen, humming to herself, 'Jingle Bells,' of all tunes.

"Well, I had better get round and do the checks," Cathy got up to leave the kitchen.

"Do you really mean it about taking us through the portal?" Eva asked.

"Absolutely," Cathy smiled back and then went out to do her visit around the workshop.

Eventually, after what seemed like hours and miles of walking, Cathy emerged back through the portal and into the cellar at the Riverside Mill.

"*I don't feel like going back to the empty apartment just yet,*" she thought to herself. "*C.J.s café it is then.*"

She wandered back from the cellar and through the maze of corridors, arriving in the main yard area and next to the café.

Sally and Oskar met her on the way and wanted a full update of the North Pole.

"Gran, is it possible for Santa and Eva to come through the portal, if I am with them?" Cathy asked.

"I have no idea, it has never been thought of before," Sally answered.

"Well, she is missing you and I suggested it. We can only try?" Cathy replied.

"I think it is a splendid idea," Sally beamed at the thought of seeing her old friend again.

"That is just what Eve said," Cathy laughed. "Anyway, I don't feel like going back to the apartment, so I am calling in the café for some food. I also want to see how the preparations for the winter solstice are coming along."

"We will walk with you," Oskar said, "I have missed you in the apartment, you have been so busy lately."

"Well, it is Silly Season," Sally teased him.

"True," Oskar grumbled, "Hurry up January, then we can have a nice quiet month."

"I hope you haven't just jinxed January. We don't seem to get any quiet months." Cathy laughed.

The trio of witch ghost and familiar walked into the café, which was quite busy. People working at the mill were in eating, some just finishing and the others about to start their shifts.

"Shall we sit near the front and people watch?" Cathy suggested.

"People watching for anyone in particular?" Oskar laughed.

"Behave!" Cathy growled.

"Whoops, yes boss, I will behave," Oskar giggled.

"Sorry, I am just tired, and everyone keeps asking me about Adam," Cathy explained.

"Order some food Cathy," her grandma advised. "Get some energy in for the last few days of madness, until next year."

"I want a quiet January and February," Cathy sighed.

"Now look who is jinxing us," Oskar laughed.

Whilst they waited for their food, the door to the café opened and young Barney came running into the café.

"Miss Cathy," he shouted out. "Look, look," and he pointed to the door.

In walked his dad, hand in hand with his mum. "Mummy can walk Miss Cathy," the small boy beamed with pride.

Mel and her husband walked over to Cathy. Mel bent down and whispered to Cathy, "The wheelchair is outside."

"Fantastic," Cathy stood and hugged Mel. "How are you doing?"

"Thanks to you, I am doing wonderful. You and your diagnosis. Dr Tom got me an appointment at the Manchester hospital. They diagnosed me with the textbook version of Myasthenia Graves: -

- Drooping eyelid
- Muscle weakness
- Trouble swallowing and speaking.
- Double vision

Absolute textbook of the rag doll disease." Mel told her. "I have to have more blood tests to look for a certain antibody and lots of nerve tests. Along with MRI and Cat scans."

'Mel was talking so much easier than last time they had met up.' Cathy thought to herself.

"She had been through a full MOT," laughed Bob. "They have said she can have an operation in the new year."

"Would that be a thymectomy?" Cathy smiled.

"Yes, the thymus gland is in the chest that forms part of the immune system. The doctor said that problems with this gland are strongly associated with Myasthenia," Bob told her.

"My friend kate had that done. Not pleasant at the time, and a long-time off work. But she just seem normal nowadays." Cathy reassured her.

"I am on lots of new medication now," Mel smiled.

"Wow, look, your smile has come back," Cathy exclaimed.

"Yes, it has. I struggled to smile because of the muscle weakness." Mel laughed, "But I can now. Without your knowledge we wouldn't be in this position now. Harold said we can rent one of the mill cottages and Bob is going back to work with Peter and Susie. We can get life back on track now."

"How is Barney?" Cathy asked.

"He is fine, I am taking him under my wing," Bob laughed. "It seems he has inherited my families magic."

"Phew, when he mentioned Clara Jane, I didn't know what to say or do." Cathy told them.

"He will start school with Donna Maria's brothers in the New Year. We thought it would be good for him to have new friends and start school with them." Bob smiled. "Thank you, Cathy."

"I was in the right place at the right time. I guess we have Tamara to thank at the end of the day." Cathy grimaced. "How is she?"

"You are an angel," Mel said. "This woman comes along a dupes your boyfriend and you ask how she is?"

"Ex boyfriend," Cathy sighed. "But what did happen to her?"

"She went on the three-month cruise like you suggested. But she cannot be with Barney alone anymore. We have a restriction order against her. She overstepped the mark and traumatised our son. he broke up you and Adam, that wasn't nice." Bob explained, "We have heard that she has met an older man on the cruise and is dating him."

"Lol no fool like an old fool, good luck to him. She doesn't waste much time, does she?" Cathy replied. "Are you coming to the winter solstice party?"

"Absolutely, now we live in the cottage, in the yard. We wouldn't miss it for the world." Mel told her.

"Coffee everyone?" Becki came over to take the orders/

"Yes please, hazelnut for me," Cathy said.

Everyone sat sipping their drinks. "Look at Barney playing happily, those are Donna Maria's younger brothers, aren't they?" Mel asked.

"Yes, they are, Nick and Neil, they have moved in with her, in her shepherds hut behind the mill, after a very difficult time with their parents." Cathy told them.

"They must be magical too, as they already go to the school." Mel queried.

"Yes, but they are new at magic too, learning slowly how to handle things." Cathy reassured her.

"The whole place is enchanted," Mel whispered.

"It sure is, Santa Season, witches, wizards, giants, fairies, boggarts, and werewolves to name a few. Although I can say, I haven't seen a werewolf yet." Cathy giggled.

"Err," Bob said awkwardly, "That is one of my families traits. I am second cousin to David and Nigel."

"Perhaps we had better get you a house in the gated community," Cathy teased.

"I have never experienced the transformation. I am more like my mother's side, a bit of a wizard I guess, if I knew how to handle it. I am thinking that is what Barney has inherited," Bob spoke.

"Who is the young girl them?" Mel asked.

"Can you see a young girl with them?" Cathy asked.

"Yes, I can, but I am not magical, so who is she?" Mel told her.

"That young girl is Clara Jane. One of the mill's ghosts. Maybe it is because you are sat with me, the local ghost whisperer, or maybe not. When you are well enough, I am getting all three of you checked over, to find your magic." Cathy laughed. "Welcome to the enchanted mill.

Chapter 21

Winter Solstice

After all the preparations for the Winter Solstice party had been completed, Cathy and Gillian had a rest before they walked back through the maze of corridors to the main yard, next to CJ's Café and the Reception block. It was only 4.00pm, when they set off, but the dusk was already turning to the black of the night.

Oskar, Hamish, and Marley were with them. An area had been set aside for all the familiars to enjoy the evening, and also any ordinary pets were welcome.

Tonight, was a celebration of the first day of winter. The winter solstice and Yuletide. After the hiccups of the recent months, Cathy was looking forward to letting her hair down and enjoying herself. Gillian was meeting her boyfriend David, and Elizabeth was meeting his brother Nigel.

Adam and Cathy were still not back together, the Tamara incident still hung in the air. Melanie, Bob, and Barney would be coming to the party, and Cathy was looking forward to the progress Melanie had made since her thymectomy.

Adam's brother Rob and his girlfriend, Liv were over from the USA, and were going to perform a few songs, on the makeshift stage that had been set up in the corner of the yard. It was there for anyone that wanted to perform, and even a karaoke machine had been set up. Cathy laughed as they passed the stage, she wouldn't be getting up and singing, she told Gillian.

Strolling into the decorated yard, Cathy saw the decorated windows of CJ's Café. They had all been covered in mistletoe, holly, and ivy. There had been a netting stretched between the room over the café, to the roof over the reception block. A thousand or more twinkling gold lights lit up the area. "Doesn't it look incredible?" Cathy and Gillian said at the same time.

Becki and Inese came over to meet them, they were still with the two Morris Men that they had met at the Upper Valley event. They were introduced has Dave and Craig.

Cathy thought to herself, about how alone she felt. *"Deep breaths she thought to herself."*

"Go and say hello to him," Gillian laughed, "he looks as miserable as you."

"Maybe later," Cathy sighed as her eyes met with Adams. She just felt that their ex-partners, and their siblings had a way of keeping them apart.

"I best get on and mingle with everyone," Cathy told the three girls.

She made her way over to see her Grandma stood with Desdemona and Donna Maria. Nick and Neil were playing football with Barney, Izaak, and Mikael.

"Look how the boys all get on together," Sally smiled. "You have done a great job Cathy."

"Thanks, Gran. Hi Donna Maria and Dessi, How have the boys enjoyed their first term at magical school?"

"They absolutely love it." Donna Maria laughed. "Especially now they are boarding. They love their lessons and mixing with the other children. Plus, the excitement of the magic lessons."

"Cathy, I heard your grandma saying how well you are doing, in your role has the head of the Coven. You certainly are an amazing woman. You have reunited my family. I never thought it was possible. But you have done so. Thank you." Desdemona wiped a tear from her eyes, as Donna Maria and the ghost of Debbie, hugged her close.

Cathy smiled as everyone was saying well done and thank you. *"If only they knew how I felt,"* she thought sadly.

Making her way to Kim and Wendy, who were in charge of the drinks table. "Hi ladies, how are you both tonight." Cathy asked them, as she helped herself to a glass of wine.

"We are great thanks," Kim chirped. "The drinks are overflowing. Both Upper Valley and Nether Valley have brought supplies of their speciality drinks." Wendy giggled.

"Oh, no. Not the juniper tea." Cathy laughed. "But not in the tea urn?"

Glynis was suddenly next to her. "Not the tea urn, sorry. We are not allowed to remove it from the headquarters. But it tastes just as good," she laughed as she refilled her glass.

"We have set the festival like food, inside the café," Kim said. "It will also create a warm indoor space for the older members of the mill."

"That is thoughtful," Cathy said. Glad she had dressed in her black velvet trousers and hoodie. Being December, it was not going to be a warm evening, as they were outside.

Cathy looked around the yard, most of the guests were already there. Drinking, laughing and above all mixing together. The vampires were chatting with the archaeologists, Ulysses and his five guards were chatting to Harold and Roger. The older members of the coven, including Betty and Cynthia were already on the juniper tea.

"Oh dear," thought Cathy. *"Sore heads in the morning."*

Liv came over and gave Cathy a big hug. "You look so sad Cathy," she told her. "He is just the same as you. Why don't you just go over and chat to him."

"It is complicated. After Tamara and my ex. I just feel I can't commit myself anymore. I love Adam, but I just feel that he no longer feels the same." Cathy confided.

"Well, shall we just enjoy the Winter Solstice without the brothers." Liv laughed, "although, Rob and I are doing a duet soon, so I will have to speak to him. But I know he does feel the same way about you. His ex-wife, your ex-husband, think of it as a test of your love and soul mate."

The late afternoon, soon turned into a dark winter evening. Gas heaters had been placed at various points, to try to keep the area warm. A bonfire wasn't possible, because of the close proximity of the mill.

The stage lit up, stage lights brightening the yard. Liv and Rob walked onto the stage, to the delight of their audience.

Cathy stood alongside her Grandma, Desdemona, and Donna Maria. The mill ghosts, Pearl and Ruby were dancing in front of the stage with Clara Jane. Even Ulysses and the guards were jigging in their corner of the yard.

They played various tunes, ones that everyone knew. Liv sang and also played the violin. Rob sang and played his guitar. People were dancing and singing along. *"Another success."* Cathy smiled to herself.

After about an hour of Liv and Rob performing, Rob announced that there would be a special performance by one of Green Valley's own famous bands.

Everyone looked at each other, and wondered who that could be. "I only know one famous band from the area. But they seem to only play in Europe these days." Cathy told her Grandma.

"Do you mean Barclay James Harvest?" Sally asked.

"Yes, although two of the original band are sadly, no longer with us. The other two members have formed their own version of the group." Cathy told her.

Kim and Wendy excitedly came over to Cathy. "Is it BJH?" Kim asked. "Oh, I do hope so."

"I haven't a clue, but look, there are some people coming onto the stage." Cathy pointed to the stage, as a lot of instruments and drums suddenly appeared.

"Ladies and Gentlemen. Please can I have your attention. For one night only, fresh from their tour in Europe and Malta. Home for the holidays, can I present to you, the John Lees Barclay James Harvest. Here to perform a few of their favourite tunes." Rob introduced the band.

Liv looked over at Cathy and said, "Cathy, you may find a tune has been requested especially for you."

Cathy felt the whole crowd watching her, yet she couldn't believe the JLBJH were actually going to perform at Green Valley.

Hush fell, everyone was in awe of the Green Valley's legendary group on a small stage in front of them.

"Good evening, Green Valley, and Riverside Mill. Thank you for letting us perform here this evening. What a setting you have here." The main man himself told the audience.

Cathy had never heard a cheer so loud, it felt like she was at Wembley Stadium, not Riverside Mill.

"Shall we start with our tune, 'Fifties Child.' In honour of the mill and all the people that worked here in in the fifties."

When the first note of the violins and guitars filled the air, everyone knew this was a very professional performance. Cheers lifted the roof if there had been one. The haunting opening of the tune, echoed in the valley air.

"*Love was a lesson we tried to learn. There were no exams to pass or fail, only heartbreak……*" Cathy listened to the lyrics and sang along. She reflected on herself and Adam. Surely, there was a reason why she was feeling this way. Maybe he was her soulmate, and this was just a test.

The bass guitarist introduced the next piece. "Out next tune will be 'Love is like a violin' For all you lovers out there.

in the audience tonight."

The music flowed around the stage and the mill lit up with the sound of music. The stage lights glowed different colours and the spotlights whirled around, sending out images of the area, making the mill wall like a huge screen.

Cathy hugged her arms around herself, as she rocked to the song being performed. "*Why wasn't she with Adam. Yes, she missed him so much.*"

"Our penultimate song is called 'Guitar Blues,' for all of you out there, that are not quite in love at the moment.

Cathy glanced over at Adam and saw him talking to Fillipe, they both looked over at her. She smiled at them both, and quickly turned her attention to the stage. "*What were they talking about?*"

"Finally, ladies and gentlemen. We come to our final song of this fabulous evening. This one is dedicated to Cathy. Not just from one man in particular, but from all of us in Green Valley and the surrounding areas. Cathy, because we all love you, this one is from Adam to you. 'Poor Man Moody Blues."

The guitars started to play; the moody voice started to sing. '*all the nights that I have missed you….*'

Cathy smiled; she loved this tune. She felt a pair of arms go around her waist and a warm kiss on the back of her neck. She leant back and felt Adam as he held her close. She heard him singing the words, and she felt the meaning in his words.

'*Yes, she missed him. Yes, she wanted him, and yes, she loved him.*' She thought.

The music continued and the pair stood as one, singing along. When the music came to an end, Cathy turned to face Adam, and planted a big kiss on his lips. The crowd erupted, as did the musicians on the stage.

Liv and Rob joined the musicians and finished the evening off with more tunes, taking the spotlight off Adam and Cathy, who were still hugging and kissing.

The evening turned into night, midnight came and went. Various others got up to sing on the stage, too much alcohol was drunk.

Suddenly, Ulysses and his five guards shouted, "Look everyone, it is snowing, our white Christmas is on its way. What a reward for all the hard work of Santa Season."

Cathy and Adam looked upwards and saw the first snow of the season falling from the sky.

Adam looked at Cathy, "Friends?" he asked.

"Soulmates," she replied.

Chapter 22

Kiss and Make Up

Cathy woke in her own bed, but she wasn't alone. She thought back to the night before and the winter solstice party. The words from the music she heard, kept running through her mind.

'Cos, I love you, cos I need you.' She thought to herself, *'yes I do love him, and I do need him in my life.'*

Cathy watched as Adam slept. She noticed Oskar had made himself scarce after the party to give the couple some privacy. Cathy snuggled herself into Adam's arms and let out a loud sigh of contentment.

Slowly waking up, Adam smiled as he saw Cathy.

"Are we ok again?" he asked her.

"Yes, I think we are." Cathy smiled and bent over to kiss him. "Do you fancy a trip to the North Pole with me, I have to go and do some final checks today?"

"You mean, go through the portal with you?" Adam grinned.

"I do. Every time I have been through, I have always wished you had been with me." Cathy admitted.

"Really?" Adam questioned.

"Of course. I have never stopped loving you. If I am honest, I just couldn't deal with Tamara, I knew she was a fake, but I didn't know how to stop her." Cathy told him.

"I could never have her back in my life. It just wouldn't work. I too didn't know how to get things sorted. I couldn't hurt Barney, even though I felt she was lying. But all the police could tell me was to track Mel and Bob on their cruise. With no law actually being broken, she was Barney's guardian whilst they had their cruise. They had left him with her in good faith, and had hoped the cruise would help Mel's illness." Adam sighed.

"Shall we put it all behind us now? Move on with our lives. I have been so busy with ghost and portals. I would love a few days in the cabin when Christmas is all over." Cathy smiled, "Our cabin."

"Yes please, I have missed our visits to the cabin. No way was I mentioning it to Tamara." Adam laughed.

"Right shall we sort some breakfast and then get on with my duties of the Protector of the Open Portal?" Cathy laughed as she raced to the shower first.

Eventually, after a leisurely breakfast, the pair made their way to the cellar of the mill.

Sally and Oskar had arrived during their breakfast, to congratulate them on the kiss and make up. As they walked through the mill, everyone was smiling and wishing them well. Clara Jane even had the cheek to say, "Two smiling faces is better than the two miserable ones we have been seeing for so long."

The couple held hands as they walked the maze of corridors to show the whole mill they had reunited.

"Have you been through the portal before?" Cathy asked,

"No, I have seen it working and the conveyor belts in place. But I have never had the opportunity to actually step through. Does it hurt?" He replied.

Cathy started laughing. "No, it doesn't hurt. I have been through almost daily. It is my duty to check in with Santa each day. I must admit I felt a bit dizzy the first time, a bit like witch flight."

"Alright, let's do it." Adam grinned.

"Prepare to be amazed," Cathy laughed as she opened the cellar door. Like always, Ulysses was at the bottom of the step waiting for her arrival.

"Miss Cathy, Adam," he bowed. "It is my pleasure to welcome you both, together."

"Thank you, Ulysses. Today, Adam will accompany me through the portal," Cathy informed him, "Ulysses?"

"Yes, Miss Cathy?" the boggart replied.

"My Grandma tells me that at the Closing of the Portal Ceremony, you accompany me through the portal, and that we go for a flight amidst the Northern Lights."

"That is what happened with Miss Sally," Ulysses replied.

"Then that is what we shall do too." Cathy told him.

"Thank you, Miss Cathy. I will look forward to that. Enjoy your day today." Ulysses bowed and then led them up the ramp towards the portal.

Cathy held Adams hand and asked if he was ready.

"I guess so," Adam laughed, "but don't let go of my hand."

"Come on, hand in hand, shall we step through?" Cathy led him to the purple swirling light in the doorway of the portal.

When they emerged through the other side of the portal, Adam let out a gasp. "Oh, my word, look at the sky. There is snow on the ground, is this real?"

"Welcome to the North Pole, The Northern Lights never cease to amaze me. Here in the North Pole, they are so much brighter than when we saw them at the cabin. The array of colours is incredible. Do you feel Ok after the portal?" Cathy said.

"I am great, wonderful, perfect." Adam bent to kiss her, just as the sleigh arrived.

"Ho, Ho, Ho," Santa bellowed, "about time!"

"Hi Santa, I would like to introduce you to Adam. My boyfriend," Cathy beamed.

"Good day young man. I am so glad you two have made up. Now jump onto the sleugh. Eva has some hot chocolate waiting for you both." Santa led the sleigh towards the workshop and house.

Still in awe, Adam whispered to Cathy, "is that really Santa?"

"Yes," Cathy whispered back. "The reindeers pulling the sleigh today are Comet and Vixen."

"Oh my, why have I been kept away from here for so long." Adam laughed.

"I would rather not answer that question," Cathy told him as she laughed, while the sleigh dashed along the snow.

First stop was to Eva's kitchen, where Adam got to try the hot chocolate and cinnamon buns. He groaned as he tasted the hot chocolate.

"How are things working out now Santa?" Cathy asked.

"Everything is packed now for the big night." Santa laughed. "The conveyor belts are saving the day, each belt loads for their own part of their countries. The reindeers are all fed and watered."

"Can we go and see them?" Cathy asked, "Adam doesn't believe me when I say they are all real."

"Stop it," Adam blushed.

"Well, I want to go and have a chat with them. I don't think I will get here tomorrow, as it is when the big night starts," Cathy said.

"Yes, Australia first and we follow the clock around the world." Santa added. "Come along then, shall we go and see to them?"

Following Santa, Cathy and Adam went from the kitchen to the barn and stable block.

"Miss Cathy," Rudolph announced, "How wonderful for you to come and visit again."

"They can talk?" Adam whispered in awe.

"Yes, we can talk, that is down to Miss Cathy's ancestor, that helped us to achieve the power of speech." Dasher replied.

"Let us introduce ourselves, I am Rudolph," Rudolph bowed his front legs, as in a bow. The rest of the reindeers gathered from their own stalls and introduced themselves to Adam.

"This is incredible." Adam laughed,

"Are we all ready for tomorrow?" Cathy asked, having to do her work whilst there visiting.

"Oh, we are always ready, it is the greatest day of the year," Rudolph said, and the others all nodded in agreement.

"Well, I shall wish you well and see you for the Closing of the Portal." Cathy told them, "We had better go and check the elves and the workshop now."

"Elves?" muttered Adam.

Moving on from the stable block, Santa led them to the workshop. Through the massive door.

"Wow, it is quiet in here today," exclaimed Cathy.

"Yes, the conveyors have stopped, only the occasional last-minute gifts to arrive now. The elves are on a break now, as everything is packed ready to go. Come and see the big sleigh." Santa led them through the workshop, out to an outbuilding.

Opening another huge door, the light came on automatically. In front of them was a huge sleigh. Full to overflowing with sacks of presents.

"Crickey, that is a big sleigh. How on earth do the reindeers pull that?" Cathy gasped.

"Oh Cathy, they haven't pulled it for years, your ancestors gave us the magic to glide through the air, at great speeds." Santa guffawed. "How do you think we get around so quickly?"

Adam was laughing, while Cathy blushed.

"Oh right, everything is magical," Cathy laughed.

"Yes, and thanks to your ancestors and you Cathy. You too are adding your own magic to the mix all the time too.

"This place is so amazing," Adam said in awe.

"Back to see Eva for some more food before you leave us. We start the big day tomorrow, and I will be going for a rest soon. We will see you for the Closing of the Portal ceremony?" Santa asked.

"Absolutely, I am bringing Ulysses, like my grandma did." Cathy said.

"Excellent, I will ask Eva to make him some supplies for him to take back to his family." Santa led the way back into the kitchen. "Eva love, Ulysses is coming with Cathy to the Closing, He will need some supplies to take back."

"Wonderful, I love that little fella," Eva smiled. "Come and sit, I have made you some lunch before you leave us."

"What is that delicious smell?" Adam asked Eva.

"My special, now eat up. Santa needs to get his rest for tomorrow. Christmas Eve for you, but with the time zones of the world, Christmas day starts at 12 noon for us, and Australia." Eva chuckled when she saw Adam tucking into the home-made stew.

"Oh, my, Cathy, you need to get this recipe, it is amazing." Adam muttered between mouthfuls of the stew. "Can we come back again, please?" His big eyes looked at Cathy and Eva, as though he was pleading.

"We are hoping to try the portal in the closed season," Cathy answered. "We have some visitors that want to visit Green Valley."

"Why would you want to leave this amazing place?" Adam questioned.

"To go and visit Sally, because ghosts cannot use the portal," Eva explained.

"Oh, now I understand," grinned Adam, "I guess it is time we made our way back then?"

"I will accompany you back to the portal," Santa said. "then I will take my rest, before the fun starts." He led them back to the sleigh, that had magically appeared by the doorway.

Cathy and Ada, left Eva and stepped onto the sleigh, snuggling under the warm blankets.

"This place is truly amazing Cathy," Adam grinned, "thank you for allowing me to come with you and to see all the wonderous things. Just look at the sky, so many shades, all we get is black grey and the occasional blue sky."

"It is my pleasure to have you alongside me." Cathy sighed contentedly, as she too, watched the Northern Lights dashing around the sky, in the rainbow of colours.

Santa waved them off through the portal, "See you soon Cathy," he called out to her,

Stepping through the purple swirling portal, Cathy, and Adam, stepped back into the cellar at Riverside Mill.

Sally and Clara Jane were with Ulysses to greet them. Sally laughed when she saw the excited look on Adam's face.

"You enjoyed it then?" Sally laughed.

"I cannot describe it Sally, except, why did you never take me through the portal?" Adam teased back.

"Because it was Cathy that took you through, she was the person meant to take you. Fate works in mysterious ways." Sally replied.

"Ulysses, next time, it will be you accompanying me, to close the Christmas portal," Cathy told the boggart.

"Thank you, Miss Cathy, I will look forward to that," Ulysses bowed.

"Right, back to the apartment for some relaxing please." Cathy told the small group.

Chapter 23

Christmas Eve

Christmas Eve arrived at the Mill, and everything seemed strangely quiet. Cathy and Adam had a leisurely morning. Cathy had finished restacking the shelves in the shop, ready for the New Year, when it would reopen. She checked her emails, and spent an hour in the Temple Room, whilst Adam went to check his house and family.

Sitting with Oskar in the Temple Room, Cathy consulted the grimoire about the closing of the portal, and trying to understand, if it could be used at other times of the year.

"It should be alright to use the portal, not in Sata Season," Oskar told her. "It is only the Christmas conveyor belts that need to be used only at Christmas."

"I hadn't thought of it that way, has anyone else been through the portal at other times of the year?" Cathy asked her familiar.

"Probably over the years, not Sally, she never trusted the technology." Oskar grinned.

"I hear that," Sally appeared in the Temple Room. "Meditate and see what the grimoire tells you."

Cathy curled up in her special seat, grimoire shining on her knee. Deep breaths and relax. Images of purple swirling mists soon filled her mind.

"Cathy, you are the portal, you are the energy to travel through. Do not underestimate your powers." The voice in her mind told her.

"*Thanks*," she thought back to her own voices. As she finished her mediation, she felt the room watching her. While she had been meditating Adam had been allowed into the Temple Room and was stood with Sally and Oskar. They were all looking expectantly at her.

"Hi," Cathy trying to wake up after her deep meditation. I appears the portal is open all year round. It is my energy that runs the portal, so I will have access to the North Pole. The ceremony for opening and closing, is linking the conveyors and Christmas present flow."

"Excellent," Adam shouted, "We can go back lots of times."

"Calm down, you're like a big kid," Cathy laughed. "Shall we all have a tea at C.J.s café, I am feeling festive now, that the Silly Season is nearly over?"

"Excellent idea," Adam agreed. They locked up the Temple Room and made their way over to the café. When they entered, they felt like everyone else was in the same frame of mind. Practically all of the coven members were in the café, old and new.

"What is happening here," she asked them, "Are we having a party?"

"We are still celebrating Yule and Christmas together, any excuse," Gillian giggled. "We did send a message, but you were busy elsewhere."

Cathy blushed, "actually I was in the Temple Room, working out how I can take other people through the portal in the closed season."

Gillian's turn to blush, "does that mean you can take other people to the North Pole? Actually, we have all just finished for Christmas and the holidays, and we all just ended up in here. Come on over and join us, tell us about the portal."

Adam and Cathy joined the group of witches, wizards, ghosts, and familiars. Becki took their orders and within minutes the hazelnut latte was put down in front of her.

Adam began to tell the gathered group about Santa and the reindeers, who could actually talk. Cathy sat and listened and smiled to herself.

"Thank goodness we are back together," she smiled to herself.

Very soon the café was full, it seemed that everyone had the same idea to spend the late Christmas Eve afternoon, at the café at the mill. Even the vampires ventured out and joined the ever-growing party.

Fillipe was the first to greet Cathy, raising her hand to his lips and kissing it. "I am so pleased you two have made up at last." His eyes twinkled with mischief. "My loss though."

Mikael and Izaac soon followed their parents into the café, followed by Tomasz and Dumar. The tables all were pushed together, creating one huge table. Everyone joined in with the impromptu party. Even the mill ghosts, Pearl and Ruby accompanied Clara Jane. Uncle John and Margaret arrived, along with Hawkeye, her familiar.

The afternoon turned into dusk, and then evening. The hazelnut latte turned into wine. The juke box was playing a variety of Christmas tunes. The children were entertained by Inese and making their own versions of Christmas Cards or Holiday cards for the ones that didn't celebrate Christmas,

"What a wonderful way to spend Christmas Eve, surrounded by family, friends and loved ones." Cathy whispered to Adam, while she looked around the people with whom she was sat.

"Look it is dark outside, shall we track Santa on his journey?" Inese suggested to the children, although the adults said yes just as eagerly.

The café emptied as everyone went outside into the dark mill yard, looking up at the crystal-clear sky.

"I have the app on my phone," Melanie showed them, "We can track where he actually is. Barney is so excited to have his first Christmas in the new house."

"Keep a look out up in the sky everyone. Look for the reindeers and Santa. The app says he should be in India, as that is six hours in front of us, timewise. Australia will be all waking up to their Christmas presents now, they are twelve hours in front of us," Cathy told the crowd.

"Will we get to see Santa," Izaak and Barney came over and each held one of Cathy's hands.

"I am not sure if we are allowed to actually see him, he is a terribly busy man, but we might see the sleigh flying high above us in the sky.

All eyes were on the dark night sky. It was a cold crisp evening, no clouds and there had been no more snow since the Winter Solstice party.

"Miss Cathy," Izaak said after a few minutes.

"What is it, Izaak?" Cathy asked the young vampire.

"I have never seen Santa." He quietly told her.

"Few children have seen the real Santa. But keep looking upwards and keep looking for something that looks like a shooting star." Cathy reassured him.

Cathy felt a warm flutter move through her.

"Crickey, was that a maternal flutter?" She thought to herself.

Time passed by, piping hot cups of hot chocolates passed around to warm up anyone feeling the cold. Just when people started to move back inside, Cathy saw a flash in the sky.

"Look, look everyone," she pointed to the long flash in the clear sky "That looks like a comet up there."

"What is a comet, Miss Cathy?" Izaak asked her.

"That isn't a comer, that is a huge sleigh, being pulled by the reindeers. Miss Cathy can explain later what a comet is." Adam laughed,

"Is it Santa and his sleigh?" Izaak asked, straining his neck to stare up in the sky.

"It could well be, if only they could fly a little close," Cathy laughed, holding back onto the two boys tiny hands.

As soon as she spoke, she could see the lights getting a lot brighter.

"Children, quick, come over here, this is a once in a lifetime chance." Cathy shouted, soon all the children from the families gathered around her, Mikael, Nick, Neil and at the front was Clara Jane.

The bright lights in the sky came closer and closer, until you could make out the outline of a sleigh being pulled by the reindeers. It did a circle about the mill.

"Ho, Ho, Ho," a huge voice boomed from above. "Hello Green valley. I can't stop just yet, but you children be good, and I will be back later."

The children waved as hard as they could to Santa, and the sleigh circles a few more times.

"Later boys and girls, and I will be back. See you soon Cathy," Santas voice disappeared as the sleigh went higher up and out of sight.

Cathy felt tears run down her face with emotion as she saw all the children's face, as they watched the sleigh slowly disappearing from view.

"Did that just happen?" Cathy asked Sally.

"Yes, it did he is a good man. He would know you were outside looking for him," Sally laughed. What did you think Clara Jane?"

"It was incredible. I feel like a young child again." Clara Jane clasped her hands to her chest in awe.

"You are a child; you are only fourteen." Sally teased.

"Yes, but I have been around for a very long time," Clara Jane laughed back.

Everyone made their way back inside the café, and eventually made their way home, with some overly excited children in tow.

The café soon was left with just a few of the coven members.

"Well Cathy, that has never happened before, Santa making a quick detour. Did you see the look on all the children's faces, and adults." Adam said.

"You're one to talk. You were all starry eyed too." Cathy teased him. "You still haven't got over your trip through the portal."

"I will confess, the trip through the portal was more than I ever imagined." Adam confessed, "You are so lucky to go through whenever you want to."

"I will take you again, I told you that before. But Ulysses is next." Cathy told him. "But look at the time, I think we should call it a night here."

"I didn't realise it was so late. Will you join me with Dad and Grandad tomorrow for Christmas Dinner?" Adam asked her.

"That would be lovely, thank you. But I have also promised Clara Jane that we will visit the graves, so she can spend some time with her family, and me with my family, you can come too if you don't mind a lot of ghosts."

"That sounds good to me too." Adam agreed. He wasn't going to let Cathy go anywhere without him,

After saying goodnight to the few remaining people in the café, Adam and Cathy sauntered back through the mill to the apartment.

"Are you sure you don't mind staying at the apartment? I don't feel up to the house yet, with Tamara being there." Cathy asked.

"As long as I am with you, I would be happy anywhere." Adam bent down to kiss her. "I love you Miss Cathy!"

Chapter 24

Christmas Day

Adam woke Cathy up with a tray of her favourite breakfast items. "Happy Christmas" he whispered gently in her ear.

"Oh," Cathy surprised to be woken, "Wow, thank you." She stretched out and slowly sat up.

"With all the hassle of lately, I am afraid to say, I haven't got you a Christmas present." Adam told her regretfully.

"Phew," Cathy laughed, "I didn't get you a present either. We will have to make do with each other."

Blushing Cathy let Adam clamber back into bed and helped her demolish the breakfast.

"What time are you out with Clara Jane?" Adam asked.

"She is having Christmas morning with Donna Maria and the boys. A proper Christmas morning for her. She didn't have many with her own family." Cathy told him. "She will arrive in an hour or so for us to go to the graveside."

"That gives us and hour or so to unwrap our presents then," Adam laughed mischievously.

Eventually the couple got ready for Clara Janes arrival, and anyone else coming with them to the graveyard.

It turned out that quite a few people were going to go and see their late deceased loved ones. Uncle John was taking Cathy. Sally and Clara jane were using witch flight, like ghosts do.

Adam and his father and grandfather came along. "Cathy, do you think we might be able to see my mum and grandma?" Adam asked her.

"I don't see why not but try not to be too disappointed if we don't." Cathy tried to warn him.

When the assembled party arrived at the graveyard, by witch flight or by car. They all assembled at the top of the steps, for Cathy to take them to their respective graves.

First of all, Cathy led Clara Jane to her parents resting place. The ghosts of her parents were waiting for her, along with the tiny child also named Clara Jane. Leaving Clara Jane, Cathy went with Sally to her own family grave. Uncle John was with Margaret, he said hello to his brother and family too.

Some deep mediation and deep breaths and finally her parents and grandparents, came clear before her own eyes.

"I have to go sort a few other people out, but Grandad Sam, could you come with me to help out. Some of these haven't seen their beloved since they passed on." Cathy greeted her family.

"Absolutely, my child, many hands make light work. Sally, I will be back to catch up soon." Grandad Sam and Cathy made their way back to Adam, Brian, and Stephen.

Cathy noticed that Brian looked quite tense. "Are you alright Brian?" she asked.

"I will be, I am worried she won't remember us." Brian whispered.

"Don't be daft dad, course mum will remember us, as will Gran. They are together in the grave just over here." Adam held his father's hand in reassurance. Stephen looked on, a bit nervous too,

"Please don't be afraid, this man with me is my Great Grandad Sam, the previous ghost whisperer of Green Valley. I took over from him, he is going to help us." Cathy told them.

Making their way to quite an elaborate gravestone, Cathy read the inscriptions, "Adam, you were very young when you mother passed, I am sorry I didn't realise."

"Don't get me started," Adam gulped, as he realised what might happen. Meeting his late mother, who died when he was just five, in a bad accident.

"Are you sure, that you want to do this," Grandad Sam asked them,

"Yes, please, do what you have to do," Brian replied.

Cathy and Grandad Sam held hands over the grave, chanting words that Adam couldn't make out.

"They have been at peace for a long while." Grandad Sam whispered to Cathy.

"We have to try, for Adam and his family. It is only fair we can reunite all that want to be."

Cathy lit a few gold-coloured candles on the grave and spread her crystals out in a grid like shape.

"Please do not be afraid, I am Cathy Collins, the ghost whisperer of Green Valley, along with my great grandfather, Sam Buckley, the previous ghost whisperer. We have Stephen, Brian, and Adam here to meet you."

"And me," a voice called from the entrance to the graveyard. Cathy turned to the voice and saw Rob, Adam's brother making his way over to them.

"Welcome Rob, just in time," Cathy smiled as the four men all hugged each other.

"I was coming back surprising you and found out you were here, I have never drove so fast." Rob told them.

"Right let me try again. Christine and Val, please can you make yourselves visible, I have your family here to meet you."

Cathy looked at Grandad Sam, and he nodded, the cold chill had arrived around them, as the two ladies began to evolve in front of their eyes.

Cathy glanced at Adam who had tears running down his face, then he noticed the others had too.

"What is going on?" the younger of the two ladies asked,

"I am Cathy Collins, the ghost whisperer of Green Valley, "I have your two grown up sons here to meet you again, Adam and Robert. Also, your husband Brian, not forgetting Stephen your father-in-law."

The older lady, Christine let out a gasp, "How have you managed this?"

Cathy and Grandad Sam explained the ghost whisperer process and as the ladies materialised from the vapour, they saw the four men stood in front of them.

"Can we touch?" Adam whispered.

"Try," Cathy coaxed him. "You have two ghost whisperers here, anything is possible."

As the family reunited, hugged, and cried, Cathy and Grandad Sam left them to return to their own family.

"You did good there Cathy my lass," Grandad Sam told her. "A right chip of the old block then."

Cathy looked around the graveyard, each family was having their own time together. *"That is what Christmas is, family. In whatever way is possible"* She smiled to herself.

Cathy's own family wanted to know what had been going on, she updated them about the portal, and how she was now back with Adam. She updated them on the museum ghosts, and the town hall sage.

Before they knew it, it was time for goodbyes again, Cathy's power was waning with all the families reconnecting.

"Don't do too much Cathy," Grandad Sam told her. "It is your energy keeping us all here. Let the others know, that you need to let us all go back for now. Now the families are reunited, it will be easier next time."

Driving back to the mill, Adam and Rob were with their father and grandfather. Cathy was with Uncle John.

"Anyone told you lately that you are doing an incredible job?" he laughed.

"A few people lately, What are you doing for Christmas dinner?" Cathy asked him.

"Oh, Margaret and I are joining you and Adam, at Brians house. I think there might be a full house." Uncle John said,

"Brilliant, I am glad we are spending Christmas together again," Cathy was genuinely happy.

"I am glad you and Adam made up, just in time, could have been a bit awkward," Uncle John laughed, as he parked the car in the car park of Riverside Mill.

The families all regrouped and walked the short distance to Brian's house, which had once been the mill managers house.

When she stepped through the door, she could smell a traditional Christmas dinner cooking. She hadn't been in this house before and was surprised at the size of the rooms, and the number of rooms. The back room was the dining room and was large enough for a huge square table that sat five or six on each side.

Adam caught up with her, "Thank you for that Cathy, it was just what dad and grandad needed."

"Who is doing the cooking?" Cathy asked.

"Oh, Kim and Wendy have been working their magic, while we have been out. You didn't think my dad was cooking?" Adam laughed.

"To be honest, I hadn't thought about who was cooking. But it looks like it will be busy and a lot of fun," Cathy held Adams hand as they walked into the lounge, and saw Harold and his brother Gilbert, from the old workhouse. Various members of the coven, Betty and Desdemona were in a corner chatting with Sally. Eric, Alf, and partners were chatting to the archaeologists.

"I think I am going to enjoy this very much," Cathy laughed when Adam passed her a champagne flute full to the top.

"Ladies and Gentlemen," Brian announced. "Welcome to our house for our Christmas dinner. Please can we take a minute to thank Cathy for all her good work throughout the year, and to wish her and Adam all the best for the New Year."

Everyone raised their glasses and cheered for Cathy. She raised her own glass, took a sip, and thanked everyone for their help to.

Eventually everyone made their way to sit at the huge table, the room was lit by candles, a huge tree glowed with many little Christmas lights.

Food was eaten, wine was drunk. The Port decanter was passed to the left, and everyone helped themselves to a wedge of stilton cheese. Christmas crackers pulled and paper hats adorned their heads.

"Happy Christmas," Adam whispered to her.

"Happy Christmas" Cathy replied, with a quick kiss on his cheek. Which was met with a lot of cheering from the other guests.

"Happy days," Cathy toasted the others.

"Happy days," they all responded.

Chapter 25

Boxing Day

Boxing Day started very slowly. Christmas Day's activities had lasted well into the early hours of the morning. Food, drink, games and a lot of love and laughter.

"What do you want to do today?" Adam asked Cathy.

"A quiet day, I have Closing of the Portal tomorrow. I am taking Ulysses with me, his annual treat apparently. He shifts into a dragon, and I am not sure I can manage that." Cathy replied.

"Why don't we go to the cabin, and then we can have a short flight, to get you back into sifting?" Adam suggested.

"Now that is what a call a good plan," Cathy smiled. "Do you fancy a quiet New Year at the cabin, just us two?"

"That is my kind of plan too. But do you really think we will be allowed to celebrate New Year, by ourselves?" Adam laughed.

"I doubt it," Cathy giggled, "But for today, shall we go and fly the valley? For tomorrow I have work to do. I will let Sally know where we are going just in case we are needed. I will tell her we will be back early in the morning."

"Excellent, I will let Eric and Alf know, just to check the cabin is habitable. I am sure Rowan and Rimmon have kept everything in order. It has been too long since we have been there." Adam sighed,

Not long after, Cathy and Adam arrived by witch-flight at their log cabin, overlooking the whole of Green Valley.

"Do you still wear the ring, to summon the giants?" Adam asked.

"Yes, I wear it all the time," Cathy showed him the emergency ring.

"Can I have a quick look at it?" Adam asked. Cathy took the ring off and let Adam have a look.

Thinking no more about it, she opened the door and went into the cabin. Everything was clean and tidy. Cathy laughed out loud, when she saw that the hot tub had been prepared and was nicely bubbling away.

"Check the fridge," she shouted to Adam, who was still admiring her ring. "I bet we have a full fridge too."

"Yes, it is full of all our favourite things," Adam grinned, and handed her the ring back. "No point wasting it, I will get the snacks ready, while you test the hot tub. We shouldn't waste our time, let's relax before we go for a flight."

Cathy walked out onto the balcony of the cabin and marvelled at the view in front of her. Her beloved Green Valley was spread out in front of her. The twinkling of Christmas lights lit the houses and streets.

She quickly changed to appropriate clothing and slid into the bubbling hot water. "*Bliss*," she thought to herself. She was already unwinding from a few seriously busy and emotional months.

Adam soon joined her, along with a selection of snacks and drinks.

"I could live here," Cathy told him.

"Again, I doubt we would be allowed, the local ghost whisperer and head of the coven is usually in demand. But no stopping us just escaping more than we did before." Adam bent to kiss her.

"How was your dad and grandad after the visit to the graveyard?" Cathy asked.

"They both seemed to have had a weight lifted off their shoulders. You worked magic for them, and Rob joining us was so special. You worked your magic on them; how can I thank you?" Adam praised.

"I am sure I can think of a way," Cathy teased him.

"Later you minx." He laughed. "What do you want to shift into for your practice flight?"

"Not a dragon, that is for sure." Cathy laughed," "That one can wait for tomorrow. Shall we do the golden eagle again? That is always so exhilarating,"

After a long relaxing soak in the hot tub, working their way through the treats and snack. Adam and Cathy left the cabin to call at the giants, to see if they too were going for a fly over the valley.

As usual, the reception from Alf, Eric, and their wives was as warm as always, and very soon, six bodies, of all shapes and sizes were flying over Green Valley.

Cathy had missed this form of freedom. The change of her body into the majestic golden eagle. To be able to fly high above the valley and onto the coastline.

"Just a short flight today, save yourself for tomorrow," she heard Adam speak telepathically.

The party flew around the boundary of Green Valley and Upper Valley. The Christmas lights flickering below them, a hint of snow on the top of the hills was a beautiful sight for them all to see,

After the flight, Eric and Alf invited them the couple for a boxing day BBQ, how could they refuse.

The balcony at the giants castle like home, had the same view as the log cabin. The friends sat on the balcony watching the late afternoon turn into evening. The lights of the houses and streets shined even brighter in the dark, like a million coloured jewels on a black backdrop,

Chapter 26

Closing the Portal

Early the following morning, Cathy and Adam closed up the log cabin, promising to be back for the New Year. But today Cathy had to go and take Ulysees thorough the portal, and then perform the closing ceremony.

Arriving back at the apartment at the mill, Cathy took a quick shower and dressed appropriately for the closing ceremony. Catching up with Grandma Sally, for advice about shifting into a dragon.

"My advice, let Ulysses shift first, and then just follow his example. I can assure you; it is nothing to worry about and it will be worth it. I do miss my flights with Ulysses." Sally sighed.

Making their way to the cellar of the mill, Cathy's nerves began to tingle in anticipation. "*I hope it all runs smoothly,*" she thought to herself.

As she walked into the room holding the portal, she could see Ulysses and his cousins stood on duty, but also the three vampire brothers were there too. "*Phew, back up is here,*" she smiled to herself.

Harold stood to welcome everyone. "Ladies and Gentlemen, and familiars, welcome to the Portal. I hope everyone has had a tremendous Yuletide and Christmas."

Lots of mummering went around the room, Cathy saw all her coven members, old and new. The she saw Ulysses being helped into a coat of many colours, it was every shade of blue, purple and red that one could imagine, with green and oranges too.

"First of all, in the proceedings, Cathy and Ulysses will take their turn through the portal for the annual dragon flight. Whilst they are away, we shall all partake in the food provided by Kim and Wendy." Harold continued. "On their return, Cathy will perform the Closing of the Portal ceremony."

Cathy stepped forward and took Ulysses unusually smooth hand, and they stepped together towards the purple swirling mist of the portal.

"Are you ready?" Cathy asked the brightly coloured boggart.

"I am Miss Cathy," Ulysses replied. "I have my special coat on ready. Your ancestor made this form me, for the very first time I was allowed through the portal."

Cathy and Ulysses stepped together and went through the portal. On the other side, Santa, Eva, and the reindeers were waiting for them.

"Welcome Cathy and Ulysees," Santa greeted them. "Another successful Christmas completed."

"Thank you for passing over the mill, you made a lot of people very happy." Cathy told him.

"For you Cathy, anything is possible." Santa made a slight bow. "Shall we head towards the clearing Ulysses?"

"Oh yes please," the boggart bounced about in his coloured coat.

"If we must," Cathy grimaced.

"It will be alright Miss Cathy," Ulysses reassured her.

Cathy looked around her, she hadn't been to this clearing before. She marvelled at the sky, the aurora borealis was in full showtime, (the northern lights), but today there were streaks of pink inside the night sky rainbows. She also noted the colours were the same as Ulysses' coat.

Santa led them to the centre of the clearing, as she got off the sleigh, Santa whispered to her, "just watch Ulysses and follow his lead." He pointed to the small boggart that was already in the centre of the clearing.

"Come Miss Cathy, it is time," he shouted eagerly.

"You first, and I will follow" she shouted back to him.

"Now just watch, it is amazing," Santa and Eva stood watching the boggart.

Cathy looked and watched him. His arms were spread out, and his brightly coloured coat seemed to be expanding, and she saw him growing in height.

"Is it me, or is his jacket growing," Cathy asked in awe.

"Your ancestors made him the coat, especially for his visits to the North Pole. Keep watching," Eva told her.

Before her very eyes, the tiny boggart began to shape shift. He grew and grew. His arms turned into wings, as he slowly transformed into a dragon. But that wasn't all, he was huge, and the colouring of his scales were the exact shade as the sky and the northern lights - Purples, blues, greens, reds, orange and even gold.

Cathy watched on in awe as the transformation completed. In front of her was a true fire breathing dragon, complete with wings, spikes, and an exceedingly long tail.

"Your turn now," Santa said, "just imagine the same sort of dragon. We will be flying alongside you in the sleigh. Off you go now."

Cathy cautiously made her own way into the centre of the clearing. She watched Ulysses flying overhead. Camouflaged in the night sky.

Taking a deep breath, Cathy concentrated on her own shift. *"Just follow his lead,"* she kept repeating to herself,

Could she really shift into a magnificent dragon too?

Concentrating hard, she felt her body beginning to shift and change. Growing, stretching, Cathy let her magic take over and do the work for her. When she finally opened her eyes, she was astounded at what she had turned into. She was the same as Ulysses, just a little smaller. She had wings, scales and also a long tail.

Gently flapping her wings, she realised she was taking off and about to soar over the North Pole as a dragon.

The huge size of the dragon felt just the same as being a golden eagle or a heron. It just came naturally to her.

"Off you go," shouted Santa, "We will follow you."

Cathy flapped the massive wings and soared high into the dark sky. Ulysses nodded and indicated that she follows him. Doing as she was told; she flew alongside the dragon that was Ulysses.

"I wish someone was filming this," she thought to herself. *"This is so incredible."*

The pair of dragons soared high, and Cathy thought of her ancestors that had given Ulysses this beautiful gift. The boggart truly deserved it, from his humble beginnings to his role of the Keeper of the Closed Portal.

He led her in and out of the light show. The colourful night sky reflecting on their shiny scaled skin.

The long pink stripes in the sky, that Cathy had seen earlier seem to take on the effect of a slalom run, and the dragons found themselves flying in and out of them.

The colours were incredible. As they travelled higher into the sky, the green aurora lights turned into different shades, the higher they went the stronger the colours. Greens, Dark reds, Blues, Purples. At the highest pointes, the aurora was delicate pink and yellows.

It felt like they were flying through ribbons of colour. A night time rainbow spread around them and circling all around them.

Ulysses ducked and dived through the ribbons. Cathy followed him and spotted Santa and the sleigh. She tried to speak, but instead a stream of fire escaped her mouth, *"Whoops, I had better be careful with the fire,"*

She hears Santa's deep guffaw as the reindeers quickly changed direction from the shooting fire.

Nothing could beat this experience, she hoped that she could share it with Adam one day. But all good things come to an end, and Cathy felt herself tiring, so she signalled to Ulysees she was heading back, but for him to carry on flying.

While she descended, she took in all she could of being up close to the northern lights. Landing quite clumsily, she took a deep breath and started the process of transforming back to her own self,

It still amazed her how it didn't hurt her body, only made her feel tired.

Santa and his sleigh landed next to her, and Eva rushed over to hug her and provided a cup of hot chocolate for her.

Sitting snuggly back in the sleigh, Cathy hugged the mug close to her, sipping the drink. She watched as Ulysses flew his final few moments.

When he eventually returned down to earth, Cathy had regained some of her energy.

"Here you go Cathy," Santa laughed, "We recorded you flying, I will send it to you over the phone, so you can show Sally.

"Oh, thank you, that's so kind. I was wishing it would be recorded, I could never explain this with just words. You are so lucky to live here in this landscape. I will soon be back to take you both to Green Valley, you deserve the break too." Cathy hugged them both,

Ulysses climbed back into the sleigh. "How did you enjoy that, Miss Cathy?" he asked as he straightened his jacket, the jacket that had just turned him into a huge fire breathing dragon.

"It was more than incredible, it was super amazing, I just can't explain," Cathy told him. "Thank you for showing me."

"You don't thank me Miss Cathy, I cannot give you enough gratitude for that experience," Ulysses took a little bow.

"Well, I suppose we had better get back to the closing ceremony, then Ulysses you can go and see your family." Cathy didn't want to leave, but she did know she would be back soon.

"Ulysses, I have a basket of goodies for your family," Eva showed him an enormous hamper.

"Thank you, Miss Eva and Miss Cathy, my cousins will be in charge of the closed portal while I am away, and Miss Eva my family will be very happy with this hamper." Ulysses lifted the huge hamper.

Stepping back through the portal, Cathy felt like she had been away for hours, yet it hadn't been long at all. Adam and Sally met then as they stepped through the portal. Adam helped Ulyssess with his hamper.

"Well, how was it?" they both asked at once.

"It was truly an experience I will never forget. I nearly burnt Santa and the sleigh, I forgot dragons breath fire," she laughed, as her phone pinged with an incoming message.

"Look, Santa filmed us," Cathy showed them the footage of her flying in the northern lights.

"Good grief, you look good," Adam laughed as he watched the two dragons soaring with the northern lights. "You won't want to be an eagle again."

"You bet I will, a dragon is an amazing experience. But when I am an eagle, I have you by my side. Maybe one day, you can be a dragon too, and fly with me through the portal."

Making everyone jump, Harold clapped his hands for everyone's attention, and announced it was time for the closing ceremony.

Cathy hurried to stand by his side and said out loud the words she had rehearsed so many times in her Temple Room.

She hears the clunk when all the mill's Christmas conveyor belts returned to their own recesses and the doors closed until next year. The portal itself seemed to go into a darker purple colour and the swirling mist turned to a more solid state.

"Have I closed it permanently?" Cathy asked Sally.

"Oh, not at all, you have just closed the Santa Season, the portal will respond to you if you want to go back through at any time," Sally told her,

"That is good, because I told Santa and Eva, I will bring them here in the New Year," Cathy laughed.

"Excellent," Sally smiled, "We can have a New Year Party."

Cathy looked at Adam and sighed, "So much for us to being alone at New Year, and it was all my own doing."

"Do not worry Cathy, we have all our lives for time to be alone," Adam took her hand, "Here comes the food, you need to restore your energy, The madness of Santa Season is behind you now, and it is time to relax."

"I do hope it is a quiet new year, and no more mayhem for a while," Cathy laughed, as she headed to the food table and to catch up with her coven members, friends, family, and familiars.

**To be continued in Book 4
Mayhem at the Mill**